THE Sound OF WAVES

A deaf teenager copes with life's challenges

Sandrene Jackson-Douglas

LMH PUBLISHING LIMITED

First Edition
10 9 8 7 6 5 4 3 2 1

Editor: K. Sean Harris
Cover Design: Roshane Mullings
Book Design, Layout & Typesetting: Roshane Mullings

Published by LMH Publishing Limited
Suite 10-11, Sagicor Industrial Park
7 Norman Road
Kingston C.S.O., Jamaica
Tel.: 876-938-0005; 876-938-0712
Fax: 876-759-8752
Email: lmhbookpublishing@cwjamaica.com
Website: www.lmhpublishing.com

Printed in the U.S.A.   ISBN: 978-976-657-079-8

NATIONAL LIBRARY OF JAMAICA CATALOGUING-IN-PUBLICATION DATA

Name: Jackson-Douglas, Sandrene, author.
Title: The sound of waves : a deaf teenager copes with life's challenges /
   Sandrene Jackson-Douglas.
Description: Kingston, Jamaica : LMH Publishing Limited, 2022.
Identifier: ISBN 9789766570798 (pbk)
Subjects: LCSH : Young adult fiction. |Jamaican fiction. | Deaf – Fiction. |
   Hearing impaired – Fiction. | People with disabilities – Fiction.
Classification: DDC 813 – dc 23

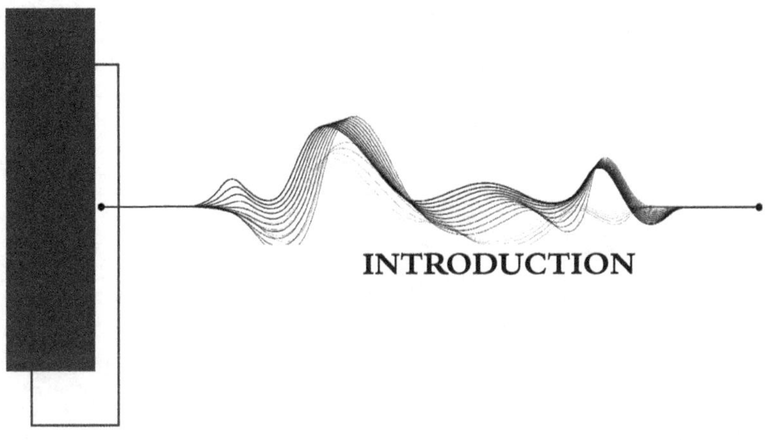

INTRODUCTION

The aim of this book is to provide affirmation for children within the deaf/hard-of-hearing community by giving them a chance to read about their reality and seeing what is common to them being depicted in fiction. It is equally important that children who are not a part of the deaf/hard-of-hearing community be exposed to the realities of children who are not like them. Additionally, I have hopes of this novel being integrated into the reading curriculum of high schools. The world is filled with people who are different and one of the best ways that schools can help to instill tolerance, is by helping students to hear the stories of those considered different.

Sandrene Jackson-Douglas

CHAPTER

1

"We are the captains of our own ships; it is us who decide how far we go."

Benjamin's mother was looking at him as if she had just told him a scientific truth. He nodded, pretending to agree with what she had said, although he was irritated by the silliness of the statement. He was tempted to make a wisecrack but he had become accustomed to his mother's self-righteous speeches, so he said nothing.

His baby brother Thomas was napping in his perambulator; the rattle of the wheels running over the crushed stones on the asphalted road were being drowned out by the cluster of student voices ahead of them. The tallest boy in the group turned around and waved politely, his smile revealed the haphazard manner in which his teeth lined his gums. Benjamin hissed beneath his breath and turned his head away as if he had not seen him. His mother smiled and waved back. He had reasons to be sure that the boy's respectful attitude was just because of his mother's presence. There were a flutter of butterflies hovering in the yard which Benjamin secretly called House-of-Flowers. It was the only dwelling in the community where you could find every variation of anthurium displayed in pots lining the walkway from the gate to the verandah. The two fluffy Maltese puppies in the yard were running and dodging beneath plant leaves and rose petals as if they were playing hide-and-seek with the butterflies. Suddenly, there were light drizzles on their faces, which caused the students in front of them to place their hands over their heads and take off running. Benjamin was excited for the sparse droplets that seemed to have come out of nowhere. He thought that this was maybe an opportunity for him to go back home and miss school for the day.

"It's just a rain shower cloud passing," his mother said, averting her eyes from the sky.

She stopped to pull the canopy over Thomas in his perambulator. Benjamin was disappointed that she had not suggested that they return home although he knew the importance she placed on school. He knew the chance of him going back home was almost non-existent. He could feel her eyes on the side of his face, but he kept his head held forward as they started walking again. The closer Benjamin got to school, the more he was sweating and leaving water marks under the armpits of his uniform shirt. He bent his arms at the elbows and positioned them like chicken wings to allow breeze to pass through the openings in the sleeves to dry them. His mother, sensing his nervousness, looked over at him and was about to say something but changed her mind and did a little cough instead.

They were passing the house on the school road which was built like a rectangular shop with its piazza front serving as a verandah. The twin toddlers were shirtless in the yard, playing with their box-made trucks at the wire fence which separated their home from the empty-lot beside the school. Their belly buttons looked like small balloons that were blown up and placed beneath the skin of their bellies. Benjamin looked at them, trying to remember if he had ever seen an adult whose shirt protruded at the navel area. Maybe he was staring too hard and it caused his mother to say, "They have umbilical hernia, they will outgrow it."

Her shoes were making grating sounds in the gravel that had been washed away from the heap on the sidewalk and had ran onto the roadway near the school gate. She clipped the brakes on the wheels of the perambulator before holding Benjamin's shoulders and turning his face to meet hers. She looked him over, examining every inch of his face. She then wet her finger on her tongue and dabbed the corner of his eyes. He would have preferred if his mother no longer did this in front of the other students because it was another thing he was embarrassed about after she was gone.

"What is your affirmation for today Benny?" Her tone had become serious.

"I am perfectly imperfect," Benjamin said.

His mother hugged him, pressing him against her chest and holding him there until he could smell the perfume that she had sprayed onto her shirt. Thomas was still sleeping, so Benjamin gently rubbed his chubby fingers before walking away. His mother stood and watched as he went through the school gate, to join the hustle and bustle of the start of the school day.

After assembly, students filed to their classrooms walking quickly to get to their seats before their teachers arrived. Benjamin was walking up the stairs when Imran joined him on the step, digging dried mucus from his nose which he flipped from his fingers to the floor tiles.

"Why must your mother do that every morning?" Imran asked.

Benjamin shrugged his shoulders in silent response and continued to walk. Imran got the message and did not say anything else about it. He slid one of his knapsack straps from his shoulder and proceeded to bring his bag forward to his stomach. He unzipped the bag and took out a *Slender Man* comic book. He then flipped open the cover page and showed Benjamin an autograph that said: *To Imran, From E. Knudsen.*

"You know who Eric Knudsen is?"

Benjamin shook his head from side to side, which caused Imran to do a little chuckle in disbelief.

"He is the creator of Slender Man," Imran said, while making small taps on the book with the back of his hand. "Mr. Knudsen signed this himself!"

He was grinning from ear to ear as he shoved the comic book into Benjamin's face. Benjamin knew that Imran was lying. It did not need a forensic handwriting specialist to see that the autograph was done by Imran himself. It seemed as if he had written the whole thing with his left hand, the curved way in which he wrote his 'I' at the start of his name could not be hidden.

"Wow! That is marvelous!" Benjamin said, trying to fake a hint of jealously in his voice.

Convinced he had managed to fool Benjamin, Imran sped away triumphantly with the comic book in his hand to the classroom. When Benjamin got to the class, Imran was embroiled in a heated conversation with some of their classmates who were chastising him about lying. Benjamin smiled and took his seat.

The morning sessions were uneventful except for Imran who was complaining to Benjamin about how foolish the rest of their classmates were.

"You are the only sensible person in this class Benjamin," he said over and over, talking in low tones from the desk behind. Benjamin could hardly wait for the lunch bell to ring so that he could escape Imran's grumbling. He was going to be alone and miserable at the tree, but at least his ears would finally get some peace.

॥⋅⋅⋅⦙⦙⦙⋅⋅⋅⦙⋅⦙⋅⋅⦙⦙⦙⦙⋅⋅⋅⦙⦙⦙⦙⋅⋅⋅⦙⦙⦙⦙⋅⋅⦙⋅⋅॥

"How's it going Benny?"

Benjamin was startled by the voice and looked up from his puzzle to see that Mr. Lewis had come to a stop by the tree. He was expertly holding a grass straw clenched between his teeth with the stalk hanging loosely from his mouth.

4

"Who do you think will win the match later?" Mr. Lewis asked.

The straw trembled with each word but was settled securely between his full lips.

"We will just have to wait and see," Benjamin responded dismissively whilst refocusing on his puzzle. Mr. Lewis stood there, looking with his arms folded across his chest as if he were contemplating what next to say. He did an awkward little chuckle and snorted, but Benjamin kept his eyes on the puzzle.

"Okay then Benny."

With that Mr. Lewis set off, wiping the lines of sweat cascading down his face with the white towel he had resting over his shoulder. He pulled his no-name goat behind him as he disappeared over the little slope between the playfield and the school building. He must have realized that Benjamin was not in the mood to talk and left him to wallow in his loneliness.

It was not Benjamin's intention to be rude, but he had too many things on his mind to be talking about a cricket match with the school's groundsman. Or maybe it was because he was so disillusioned with his own life, he would rather not deal with Mr. Lewis' gentle voice and bright personality. No one had ever seen Mr. Lewis upset, not even that time when someone had the audacity to uproot all of the orchids in his little garden and trample on them. He only stood pensively, staring at the ruin and muttering, "God knows best" to himself.

Whenever Mr. Lewis was not too busy, he would set his tools down and join Benjamin under the tree for match day cricket analysis. He had a repertoire of cricket stories too. He once showed Benjamin the picture album he had compiled of Sir Vivian Richards in his heyday. The album was wrapped in several sheets of dated newspapers, which he placed in his lap and unwrapped tenderly. He spoke in low tones as if he was afraid of his voice being too rough and would rip the pages into shreds. He patted his finger on his tongue before turning the heavy paper on which the photos were glued. He flipped through each page, explaining when and where the photo was taken as if he was the photographer, although Benjamin had seen that they were mostly cut from old newspaper articles. The pride of the album was on the last page, like a grand finale. It was a glossy photograph of a much younger, and more handsome Mr. Lewis posing side by side with Sir Viv Richards at Sabina Park in the 1980s.

The limbs from the massive tree were blocking the direct sun rays that brought the unbearable heat. From the hill, the orange sun looked like a painting against the royal blue waters of the Caribbean Sea. Benjamin took a drink from his water bottle and opened the container bearing his corned beef sandwiches. He used a small stone to weigh down the empty paper bag beside him on the root of the tree. The peals of laughter were getting louder and he stared with longing at the other students running and screaming on the playground. He would have preferred being with them, but thinking about his pride, he remained at the tree eating his sandwiches. This was his escape, one of the few places in the school where he felt safe and would not be bothered by his tormentors.

Mango was in season and the sweet juice from the fallen fruits had rightly attracted a multitude of fruit flies, bees and ants. In his solitude, Benjamin had somewhat demystified the insects. He had observed that they were complicated beings, their ways of doing things were not without intention. He especially liked to observe the careful movement of ants, how they seemed to have a language unknown to humans, walking in perfect form, never breaking the order of the lines. In his next life, he hoped to be an ant; at least he would have a purpose and be included.

He was bent over dropping crumbs of bread on the ground when a small green tennis ball brushed past his leg before getting hitched in a tuft of signal grass growing in the shade of the tree. A girl with olive-brown skin and pigtail braids darted past him to retrieve it. She picked up the ball and brushed off the loose grass that had attached themselves to its furry exterior. She glanced at him each time before throwing the ball in the air with great effort, and watched in anticipation as it went higher and higher. She did this maybe six or seven times, opening her mouth and flailing her arms each time as the ball descended from the air. Benjamin had covered his face with his puzzle book, but he was coyly following her movements from the corner of his eyes, not wanting to make it obvious that he was watching her.

"Hi, I am Lanay."

The girl had abruptly stopped her game of throw-up-and-catch and was staring at him. They were the only ones at the tree, but that did not stop Benjamin from foolishly looking around to see if anyone else was there. She was standing next to the pile of fallen mangoes Mr. Lewis gathered every morning to feed his goat. She became bright eyed; bothered by the insects flying around and swung her arms wildly to shoo them away.

"I... I... I am Benjamin, but everyone calls me Benny," he stammered.

He closed the dish with the remainder of his sandwich and placed it inside the brown paper bag. A mango became detached from its stem, rattled through the leaves and landed in a loud putt on the ground in front of her. She opened her mouth and placed her hand over her heart as if hearing a fruit falling was unfamiliar to her. He did not say anything, in fact, he welcomed the distraction. He stared at Lanay blankly, a sort of restlessness had started to possess him. He was so accustomed to being alone that her presence made him unsettled.

"I thought you were sleeping," she said, while stomping her feet on the ground to get rid of the ants that were crawling over her shoes. "I was shouting for you to stop the ball and you did not move." She giggled a little before resuming her game. He was not sure if she was expecting an answer.

The background noises from the other students happily engaged in play was affecting his hearing. He did not sense anyone approaching nor did he hear her asking him to stop the ball. Her presence made him uncomfortable and he sat there unsure of what to say. She resumed tossing up the ball, but this time she had challenged herself to clapping three times before she caught it.

Benjamin had seen her around a few times before, though they had never spoken. He had thought how small she seemed for grade seven. She had a round baby-like face with piercing grey eyes and spoke with a slight accent. It was the third quarter of the school year and he thought it rather odd to be starting a new school at that time. Rumor had it that her father was a secret agent who had fled to the island. At least that was what Imran had told him.

"Not going to play?" she asked, pointing to a group of boys in the distance huddled over a game of marbles.

"I don't feel like it," Benjamin responded.

He had been asked that question many times before and had already prepared himself with an answer. He did not want her to know that he was not welcome to play with them. He had even been rejected from cricket games although he was a top-notch cricketer. He did not want her to know that he had a closer relationship with insects than he had with humans who were not in his family. He did not want her to know that he did not stop the ball because he did not hear her asking him to.

Lanay was edging closer to the tree root. She had stopped her game and the ball was once again laying in the tuft of grass. An unmovable lump, about the size of a dumpling, was formed in his throat despite his many attempts to swallow it. He moved over on the elevated root of the tree, sliding his palms over its rough bark as Lanay invaded his space. She complained briefly about the squashed mangoes on the ground attracting the swarm of flies whirring around.

"Did you catch the final episode of Angelic Voices last night?" she asked. "I still think Penny has a better voice and should have won."

She had barely sat down before she started asking him questions. Their first meeting was not going the way that Benjamin would have wanted. Lanay was a chatterbox and she was not shy about it. She reached inside her tunic pocket and took out a small packet of gummy bears. He watched as she used her fingers to remove all of the yellow bears, placed them in her left palm and handed him the remainder in the bag.

"I did not remember to watch," he said.

"How could you forget something as important as that?" she asked.

She looked at him as though he had committed an unforgivable act. He had remembered perfectly but he did not care for silly singing shows. Benjamin did not want to offend Lanay by telling her that he felt that singing shows were silly. He felt more comfortable making an excuse than outwardly expressing his dislike for the show. He tossed candy into his mouth and looked over at her, silently admiring the comfort with which she spoke. He did not know what to make of her. She was slowly chewing on the gummy bears and swinging her feet as the leaves rustled above their heads.

As Lanay was about to speak again, the bell rang signaling the end of lunch break. Benjamin was grateful. He found her to be a bit inquisitive and was relieved to be escaping her intrusion. But he had other reasons too to be relieved. He did not want her to notice his hearing aids and know that he could not hear without them. He did not want her to immediately think that he was a spectacle who belonged in a circus.

Benjamin thought that the hearing aids were both a blessing and a curse. He could hear with them, but the stares and questions they would cause sometimes made him question if they were worth the trouble. Last year he did a whole exposition on his severe hearing loss for his end-of-term social studies project. He had explained that being deaf meant that he must wear hearing aids to help him to detect sounds, and also help him to speak along with speech therapy. He drew a picture of himself holding his ears to explain why the hearing aids were not always helpful, especially when there were too many differing background noises in his environment. He would become very confused and find it hard to concentrate.

They took up their belongings and walked back to their classrooms in silence, neither of them knowing what to say to the other. Lanay was biting down on her bottom lip, her eyes narrowing as if she was deep in thought. Benjamin was uncomfortable in her company and hoped that she would not make it a habit to come to the tree. It was his tree, it was where he found comfort, it was where the insects had accepted him. They had taken the short way up the northern staircase which led directly to his classroom. As a parting indication, he gave a brief nod and she smiled, displaying two rows of perfectly aligned teeth before he disappeared into his classroom.

A smile crept across his face when he remembered that school was going to be dismissed two hours earlier to facilitate a teacher's workshop. As the thought filled his mind, his feeling of happiness was immediately replaced by crippling fear. He remembered that his mother would not be able to meet him at the school gate for them to walk home together. He had to walk home by himself and spend the afternoon at the neighbour's until she got home. His fingers immediately began to get cold and wrinkly at the tips as if they had been soaking in water.

"Where is Houdini when I need him?" he mumbled to himself.

It was going to require one of Houdini's greatest magic tricks to get him out of the situation that he suddenly found himself in. Ms. Samuels raised her head from the name register to look at him standing at his desk.

"Did you say something Benjamin?" Ms. Samuels asked as he pulled out the chair and took his seat at the front. She walked over to him and started brushing bits of dried leaves from his hair and shoulders. Her oval shaped glasses lens glimmered from the light entering the room through the square windows overlooking the eastern side of the compound.

"No… no… no ma'am," he stuttered. He always stuttered when he was nervous, and he hated it.

The realization that he would be on his own after school suddenly casted a burden upon him which made it impossible for him to concentrate. Ms. Samuels had given out a worksheet with fractions. He had practiced every night before bed and knew how to simplify even the most difficult fraction by heart, yet he was making a lot of mistakes and was becoming impatient with himself. Benjamin rested his head on the table and covered his face with the worksheet. Ms. Samuels thought his abrupt inadequacies in the lesson was a result of his seating, and offered for him to sit at her table so that he could better concentrate. Since kindergarten, he has always had to sit at the front of the class where he was able to read the lips of his teachers and pay attention to gestures. His seating was fine, but he dared not tell her that she possibly would be attending his funeral soon.

The dismissal bell was met with jubilant shouts of yeah, which echoed throughout the school. It was almost as if the screams were being carried by the wind. Benjamin was a mixture of emotions. He was happy that he got to go home early which meant that he could catch the final moments of the one-day test cricket match between the West Indies and India on television. On the other hand, he knew that walking home without the protection of his mother would mean that his bullies would eat him alive. He dawdled about the classroom, making slow movements to gather his belongings and place them in his bag. Ms. Samuels stood at the door, constantly checking her watch and then looking at him, wondering what was taking him so long. There was nothing Benjamin could do, he had to leave so he mustered the strength, took up his brown paper lunch bag, slung his knapsack over his shoulders and headed towards the school gate.

The electronic gate rattled open and he felt like he was stepping out of a palace and into a jungle. There would be no cameras or teachers to offer any sort of protection. He forced himself to think good thoughts as his mother would always encourage. He could almost hear her voice in his head echoing, "Benny you are smarter and braver than you think."

He started to hum a tune, trying to erase all thoughts of the certain death he had been harbouring in his head. He could see Norman and his followers from the corner of his eyes buying peeled June plums in bags with salt from the cart-vendor who had brought his cart to a stop under the 'no-vending' sign hammered into the school's perimeter wall. He faked confidence and started his journey. His house was not too far away, but when your life was on the line, even a one-minute walk could seem like an eternity. Maybe it was destiny, or pure bad luck, but it did not take long for Benjamin's tormentors to realize that he was without the protection of his mother on which he had become dependent. There were hushed giggles when the prickly core of a June plum zinged past his head and landed in the road. He held his head forward and quickened his pace, hoping they would not keep up. His quest to get away increased their desire to cause him anguish and they started chanting, "Baby Benny needs his mommy."

The tall boy who his mother had waved to in the morning, changed his voice and was crying like a baby. The others became energized by his creativity and in no time, Benjamin was being followed by a chorus of baby crying teenagers. He reasoned that words were just wind; he ignored their taunting and tried to walk faster. The group of boys started to walk faster and changed the words of their teasing.

"Benny is a dummy!"

"Benny is a dummy!"

They were saying it in a sing-song way which annoyed him and made it hard for him to breathe. It was like they were using those words to wrap around his neck and choke him. The afternoon was warm, but his blood felt icy cold and his mind was daring him to do what he knew he could not do. The taunting continued and Norman and his followers began to laugh loudly, which made Benjamin even more upset. It was the kind of upset which made him want to curl up into a ball and cry. He was scared. He tried to walk a bit faster but the faster he walked, the faster Norman and his minions walked. They were singing even louder which made Benjamin feel strangely alone in the world.

He was tempted to turn around and scream at them from the top of his lungs. He wanted to say, "I MIGHT BE DEAF BUT I AM SMARTER AND BRAVER THAN YOU THINK!"

Benjamin's face was reddened by anger and more than anything, he wanted to hurt them. But he could not because it was only him and there were five of them. His mother had her preachy ways about her, but she also had a sensible way of dealing with things. One thing she would always tell him was that he should never react to the foolery of others.

"Benny is a dummy!"

"Benny is a dummy!"

The taunting continued. He could not control the words coming from their mouths, as painful as they were. He followed his mother's advice and did not react to their mocking. Although, in that moment he wished he had the strength of Hulk Hogan to punch Norman into outer space, but he did not have the muscles like Hulk Hogan. He could only hang his head and continue his walk of shame towards home. At least this time Norman did not feel like showing off his superior strength by getting physical with him.

The last thing Benjamin was expecting happened. His father's blue Honda came bouncing up the road leaving a trail of dust behind. He was pleasantly surprised as the car came to a stop at the House-of-Flowers. His mother was in the front seat motioning for him to get into the car. His father rolled down his window and shouted "Benny!", revealing his wide gap-toothed smile. He felt a joy in his stomach as he glanced over at Norman and his followers, whose actions had become crippled by his parents' presence.

His parents could not have arrived at a better time and he used the opportunity to show Norman what he was made of. He looked over at the car; his mother had turned around to attend to his baby brother fussing in his car seat. His father was not doing anything, but he was not looking in his direction. Benjamin quickly brought his hand up to his face and closed his fingers and thumb over his lips. He then dashed across the road to the waiting car. He stuck his head from the open window and flashed a mocking smile at Norman as his father drove away. It was obvious that he was telling Norman to shut up, which no one else in the school had the boldness to do. He was pleased with himself; it was the first time he had the courage to stand up to his bullies. It was a nervous victory, but it was a victory none-the-less. He knew that he would eventually have hell to pay. Norman would be coming for his head.

enjamin loved school but he also hated it. School for him meant that he got to do mathematics, but it also meant that Norman, with his size of Goliath, tormented him to no end. But today was going to be a special day. Mr. Phillips, the principal, had told the students that they were going to be having a special visitor instead of one of the usual motivational speakers. There were many whispers about who it would be. Imran said he overheard Ms. Samuels telling Mr. Thorne that the prime minister would be coming. Benjamin knew better than believing Imran's story. It was the same Imran who had told him that he once saw a mermaid perched on a rock, combing her hair at the Rio Minho River when he went to stay with his auntie in Clarendon. He sometimes wondered if Imran understood that being deaf did not mean that he was stupid. He would tell Benjamin the most bizarre stories in his usual way of using his finger to dig into his nostrils as he spoke. Although he was well known for his tall tales, Imran was one of the few people who was nice to him, so he tolerated his stories.

There was a slight brush on Benjamin's shoulder and when he looked up from his puzzle, Lanay was standing there. Her trademark pigtails tumbled over her small shoulders and were tied with blue ribbons. Her round face illuminated with sweat in the afternoon sunlight. Ever since their first meeting, she would bring herself to the tree and not ask his permission to sit. He did not have a say in the matter; she had quickly acquired the position of his best friend in the school.

"Benny aren't you going back to class?"

"Oh yes, I'm coming."

The bell had rung but he did not hear it. He did not even hear Lanay coming back from the bathroom. She walked past where he was sitting and went to pick up her lunch bag that she had left laying in the dirt. The batteries in his hearing aids had gone dead and it was difficult for him to hear anything. His severe hearing loss rendered it impossible for him to hear many sounds without his device. Without his hearing aids, he could only hear very loud speech or very loud sounds such as thunder.

He had not reached his goal of completing the challenge in his Sudoku puzzle, but he was out of time. He folded the puzzle book disappointedly and placed it inside his shirt pocket. He took a quick drink from his water bottle and ran to join Lanay who had started walking ahead of him. It had almost been two weeks since their first meeting and she had not noticed his hearing aids, because she never mentioned them. She had never stared at his ears until he became flushed with embarrassment, nor had she ever asked him the dreaded question of what was wrong with his ears.

They walked along the foot-beaten path which led from the playground to the school building. Hummingbirds were getting nectar from the petunias in the little garden at the side of the schoolyard that Mr. Lewis was so proud of. The goat was close by munching on food peels Mr. Lewis had gotten from the canteen. Benjamin walked with his head down, watching Lanay's feet take rhythmic fast paced steps across the red dirt before she tapped his shoulder once again. Her face lit up with the anticipation of telling a story.

"Last night I hid in the bushes and frightened the socks off my neighbor."

He imagined the unsuspecting neighbor jumping out of her socks and started to laugh. She laughed too. Her deep-set dimples seemed to be doing a little dance every time she giggled. After the laugh, they were once again left in silence. One of her blue ribbons became undone by the wind, and instead of retying it, she pulled it from her ponytail and shoved it inside her pocket.

"Who do you think will be the special guest today?" Benjamin asked as they walked past a group of girls who had stopped by the hibiscus plant to get flowers for their hair.

He knew that she was just as clueless as he was, none of them knew who was coming. He had asked because he had nothing else to talk about and did not want to walk in silence. Also, he felt as if it was his turn to say something. He had come to value Lanay's friendship, but still got nervous sometimes when he spoke to her because of her mature ways.

"I don't know Benny, maybe it will be a celebrity. An international star like Millie Bobby Brown or Rihanna." With that Lanay chuckled. She knew the ridiculousness of her answer and basked in her own humor. Neither of them had ever seen a local celebrity, moreover an international one.

He could not help but stare intensely at her as she spoke. He was hoping that she would not notice, but in true Lanay fashion, she noticed everything.

"Is something on my face?" she asked.

She was using her hands to fervently wipe her mouth and cheeks. He felt embarrassed at causing her unease because of his own imperfection.

"No, your face is fine."

"Quit eyeballing me then," she replied with a laugh.

He was staring at Lanay awkwardly as she spoke, not because he was a weirdo, but without his hearing aids he had to lip read. Luckily, he had extra batteries in the supplies bag that Ms. Samuels kept for him in her top desk drawer, he could change them when he got to class. Hopefully before the surprise guest arrived.

Adults could be very pretentious, and Ms. Samuels was being very pretentious when he got to the classroom. She was trying her best to behave as if it was business as usual. With perfectly lined rows of chairs, freshly cut flowers in a vase that she had borrowed from the principal's office and a pristine floor, it was obviously not business as usual. For some reason, the whole class took on her pretentious mood. Benjamin asked her permission to retrieve the replacement batteries from her drawer, and quickly changed them at her desk. She was sitting in for the social studies teacher who had left instructions on the board for the students to turn to the chapter on ancient civilizations in their textbooks. Learning anything was the furthest thing from their minds, but they kept their books open, pretending to be interested in the fact that Mayans believed in hundreds of gods who controlled their lives.

Willie peeked through the window and exclaimed, "He is coming, he is coming!" They all rushed to look, only to be disappointed that the only person in the hallway was the cleaning lady carrying a bucket with cleaning supplies. Willie delighted in his cunningness by laughing loudly while clutching his belly bottom. Ms. Samuels cautioned them about their behaviour, and they took their seats, burying their heads once again in their books.

When the guest walked in, the silence that fell on the classroom was so heavy, it could be cut with a knife. The eyes of the students brightened, and their hearts throbbed with happiness. It was Benjamin's first time seeing someone who was always on television and he was amazed that the television screen did not make him seem any different than he really was. Benjamin's dream–like state reminded him of the time he partially wet the bed because he dreamt that he was emptying his bladder into the toilet. He gave himself the slightest pinch on his forearm to confirm his wakefulness. He rubbed his eyes and tried to blink away the deception they were placing before him. Each time he opened them he could not believe their good fortune. It was Paul Dore! The great Paul Dore! The great musician Paul Dore!

Ms. Samuels stood beside the guest, doing her pinched smile by squeezing her lips together to make a pout. They all knew him. In their teenaged world, Paul Dore was like a god. He had a voice so smooth it sounded as if he fed on honey throughout the day to keep his voice faultless. To Benjamin, the world had two sets of people: lucky people like Paul Dore who only good things happened to, and then you had others like him, Benny, who only knew misfortune. There was quiet chatter throughout the room as the students began to recover from their shock.

Students from other classes were bundled outside the classroom, trying to get a peek of Paul Dore through the openings in the windows. The strong scent of aloe vera floated in through the window above Benjamin's head. He eased out his chair and peeled his eyes through the window to see an older girl applying a clear gel from a bottle to her face. The scent bothered him, and he had to use his fingers to bring his nostrils together to prevent himself from sneezing. The window watchers did not stay for long. They scattered at the sight of VP Doyle's dog bounding down the hallway, alerting the crowd of his impending arrival. Benjamin stared at Paul Dore, wondering how he got to be so great. He always wondered how people made themselves great.

"Class, this is Mr. Paul Dore and …"

Ms. Samuels was using her best speaky-spokey voice to introduce him, but she would have been better off talking to stones. The students nodded vacuously in response to whatever she was saying in a show of respect. She often entertained them with her own stories, but today they wanted to hear from Paul Dore. The follicles on Benjamin's arms became elevated, forming goosebumps which resembled the skin of a plucked chicken. He took a deep breath, then exhaled slowly, trying to bring calmness to his nerves.

"Education is the greatest tool you can ever have," Paul Dore stated.

Benjamin's father had said those words to him many times before, but today they sounded like gospel coming from Paul

Dore's mouth. As he spoke, he paced from one end of the classroom to the other, like a preacher delivering a sermon on a pulpit. His feet connected with the leg of the teacher's table which caused the vase to overturn in the middle of the table. Water was seeping down the edges and some had gotten beneath the piles of books and paper. In quick movements he grabbed the vase and the bruised looking flowers, but the damage was already done. Ms. Samuels, still doing her pinched smile, took the vase from his hand and used napkins to dry up the water from the table and off the ground. Paul Dore's accident made Benjamin realize that he was not so lucky after all and bad things happened to him too.

Benjamin's hands trembled when Paul Dore opened his bag and handed him a packet of pamphlets with the words, *'If I Can, Then You Can'* written on the front in fancy cursive letters. He took the pamphlet on top and passed the others to Imran behind him. He turned the glossy pamphlet over and over in his hands, hardly believing he was touching something Paul Dore had once touched. He wanted to put the paper to his nose to find out if the insides of Paul Dore's bag smelled like the cologne he was wearing. As Paul Dore spoke, you could have heard a pin if it fell; they were starstruck.

Since he walked in, Sofia had been using her hand to fan her face while whispering, "Oh gosh! Oh gosh!" in a trance-like state. Her voice was not loud enough to disturb what Paul Dore was saying, but her action was in contradiction with her quiet, blank demeanor during class lessons. Ms. Samuels started to stare at her as if she was on the verge of asking her to leave the classroom. Sofia, sensing what was about to happen, retrieved her asthma pump from her bag and took two small puffs before placing her shaking hands over her opened mouth.

"My tests have now become my testimonies," Paul Dore said proudly.

Benjamin sat upright with his elbows resting on his desk, and his hands clasping his jaws. Before his little accident with the table, Benjamin could not imagine Paul Dore ever facing a challenge in his whole life. He examined Paul Dore silently with his eyes, feeling happiness at knowing that despite Paul Dore's fame he was just an imperfect human being. Everything about him had seemed so perfect to Benjamin.

Without warning or reason, Melody suddenly started wailing. It was an eerie prolonged wail that got the attention of everyone. She had the puzzling need to always be the center of attention. Melody was what you could call extra. She was always so extra about everything. Last summer she travelled on an aeroplane for the first time, and she went through great pains to let everyone know it. A frightened Paul Dore held his mouth open and slowly stepped backwards from the desks until his back was against the whiteboard. Willie, the class-clown, gave out a throaty giggle which was immediately subdued by Ms. Samuel's deadly stare before everyone else started to laugh. Ms. Samuels made her way to Melody's desk and quietly whispered in her ear. She instantaneously calmed down. It was like Ms. Samuels had flipped a switch and turned off her waterworks. Just when they thought she was satisfied with her two minutes of fame, she raised her hand and went in for the overkill.

"Mr. Dore I am sorry for disturbing your presentation but when you said test, it reminded me of my cousin's dog that I played with when I travelled in the aeroplane last year. The dog's name is Tess and I miss her so much."

Her puppy-dog eyes welled up with tears and were on full display. That was the thing with Melody; it was hard to decide if you were going to love her, hate her, or just pity her.

Melody's nonsense was not enough to spoil their mood. Their excitement went into overdrive when Ms. Samuels announced that Paul Dore would be giving the whole school an impromptu concert in the auditorium, but they had to be on their best behavior. Their already hushed whispers became even quieter; this was a once in a lifetime opportunity and they could not blow it. They could not believe their luck as Paul Dore left their class for another.

Each grade filed out of their classrooms in perfect lines, being excited and controlled all at once. As soon as the students got to the door of the auditorium, they scattered like fire ants on a mission. The large room was filled to the brim with enthusiastic students. Loud laughter and expressions of joy echoed throughout the waiting crowd. Benjamin was looking for Lanay but he had no luck amidst the thick gathering. He moved closer to the cement windows on the right side of the auditorium to get some of the cool air rushing up the hills. Teachers were strolling around leisurely; they were just as anxious as the students to see Paul Dore perform.

Benjamin saw Norman coming but he could not move. His ill-proportioned frame came bursting through the thick crowd, walking as if his upper body was too much strain for his skinny knock-kneed legs. He had Benjamin cornered. He smiled wickedly as he edged closer, and without a word, there was a jab to Benjamin's rib. The jab felt like he had glued a sharp blade to his elbow and had used it to tear Benjamin's rib cage wide open.

"Deaf boy you better watch yourself," Norman said, before casually walking away.

The pain left Benjamin incapable of doing anything. He grabbed his rib, bent over, and screamed at the top of his lungs although not a sound left his shaking lips. His head became dizzy and Benjamin tried to focus his eyes on the spinning black and white auditorium floor tiles. He knew Norman was not finished as yet; he was going to come back for more at another convenient time. This was just a taste of what was to come.

When Paul Dore appeared on the stage, the screams were deafening. Benjamin straightened his back just in time to see him raise his right hand and bounce it like an opera conductor to cue the music. The vibrations from the beat felt heavenly as it seeped through Benjamin's flesh and reached for his heart. The jab from Norman was now merely a prickling feeling in his rib. Norman had attempted to ruin Benjamin's afternoon, but Paul Dore was about to save the day. His voice was so powerful,

Benjamin soon forgot all about Norman. He rocked his head as Paul Dore performed his favorite song, Magical Man, and sang along with the words as best as he could.

I am a magical man
I am magical because I am strong
Life couldn't break me
Challenges never phased me
I am a magical man.

CHAPTER

3

When Winter's face came on the phone screen, Benjamin was beyond happy to see her. He loved talking to her because they were almost the same age – she was only eleven months older – they both wanted dogs, and she was deaf too. She had been upset with him for the past two weeks just because he made a simple joke. He had innocently told her that it made no sense that her name was Winter when they only experienced summer in the tropics. What had made it even funnier was that he found out that her full name was Winter Joy Dayes. He could not stop laughing after he called her Summer Sad Nights. She did not take kindly to his teasing and disconnected the call. He knew then that he had to be careful with jokes about her name.

"Hello," Winter said by extending her fingers and crossing her thumb in front of her palm, and then moving her hand outward from the side of her face.

"Hello Winter," Benjamin signed back.

That was one thing not many people knew about him. Not that it was a secret, but he thought it would not have made a difference if people knew or not. He could speak with his hands.

"My father bought me a dog," she signed.

"What breed is it?" Benjamin signed back, trying to form a smile to conceal the jealousy in his heart.

With the biggest smile, she responded, "It is a Boston Terrier."

He wanted to see the dog, but Winter said it was sleeping. He was not sure what a Boston Terrier looked like, but it sounded like one of those small exotic dogs. The kind that rich people brought to the vet and fed a special diet. He wanted a dog too, but his parents did not think that he had the maturity to take care of a pet. Even if he should get a dog, he did not want a little flimsy show-dog like a Boston Terrier, he wanted a powerful one like a Cane Corso or English Mastiff. With a dog like that, Norman would be scared to even think about touching him, he thought.

Winter ran her fingers through her hair as she delved into conversation about how annoying the popular girls at her school were. Benjamin could not help but notice how different she looked. That is the mystery of girls, he thought, there are some days they just look different. Her way of speaking had also changed, in a way she was not talking like a regular fourteen-year-old, the way he was accustomed to her speaking. The words, and the way that she had begun to express herself were different from the Winter he knew. She still used sign language, but she was beginning to use more oral language as well. They were constantly back and forth between both languages, although Winter sometimes did both together. Benjamin was concerned, he always looked forward to signing with Winter, so in a way, he felt as if she was becoming too oral. Winter had become so new, the newness made it hard for him to concentrate on the conversation.

"Benny I just can't stand those highfaluting girls," Winter said.

There she was, using another strange word; *highfaluting*. He had no clue what the word meant, but he guessed that it was not pleasant. He nodded and pretended that he understood her grief, but he was too busy thinking about ways he could convince his parents to let him get a dog. He was taking a big gulp of orange juice from the cup he had beside him when he became choked by the juice and began to cough violently. There was orange liquid spewing from his mouth and nostrils, and his eyes became watery. Winter found this hilarious and they both had a good laugh until her mother called her name from the background, reminding her that it was time for her to leave for dance rehearsals. Winter opened her palm, and waved goodbye before disconnecting the call.

Ah Ah! It was the hair! Winter had straightened her hair! That was why she had looked so different. By the time Benjamin made the discovery, Winter was long gone and must have been disappointed that he had not commented on her new appearance. He hoped she would not hold it as a grudge against him when he saw her the following day at the Deaf Retreat. The Deaf Retreat was an annual event held in Kingston. It was the only retreat of its type on the island where people with different degrees of hearing loss could come together and have fun in an environment for them.

Although they did not always agree on everything, Benjamin loved the friendship he held with Winter. She understood him. She understood deaf culture. If no one else understood, Winter did. When he told her about the problems he was having with the bullies at school, especially Norman, she tried to console him by telling him that they were just jealous. They were jealous because he was smart and had a special language. She liked to believe that they were just like the Navajo code talkers who used their special language to help the United States Marines during World War II. With Winter, Benjamin had someone to speak this mysterious language with; she did not judge him for his hand movements, funny facial expressions, or body stance. He could always be Benjamin Morgan when he was speaking to her. Like him, she attended an inclusive school and was the only deaf student at her school.

Benjamin saw her before she saw him. "Man, she has gotten taller," he whispered to himself. "She even looks taller than me."

Winter was standing at the fabric booth wearing a knee-length bright yellow dress with daisy patterns. Wisps of her newly straightened hair blew about in the light March breeze. She almost looked pretty. She did not look pretty because he knew Winter better and knew that she detested the idea of being girly and pretty.

"Winter!" he called out to her.

She immediately turned around and said, "Benny" as if she had been anticipating his arrival.

It had been a year since they last saw each other face to face and the reunion was pleasant. She gave him the biggest bear-hug ever known to mankind and rubbed the top of his head like adults would normally do to children. She smelled of perfume, not the cheap kind that smelled like roach spray, but really nice floral perfume. He could not stop staring at her. There was just something about Winter that made her seem much more mature than she was last year. Maybe it was the bright orange nail polish and the pink lip tint that she was wearing. He was tempted to comment on her 180 degrees transformation from Tom-Boy-Winter to Top-Model-Winter. However, his better judgement kicked in. He noticed she had gotten new hearing aids too. She had gotten one of those discreet receiver-in-canal kinds which was not noticeable unless you were really looking for it.

"Ohhhh, I love this song!" she shrieked.

Before he could respond, she started dancing and mouthing the words to Beyonce's *Run the World*. The music was loud and could be heard from everywhere which gave the venue a very laid-back feeling. Winter was doing a funny little dance, swaying her waist effortlessly with both hands on her hips. Benjamin thought that she looked awkward dancing.

It was hot, but not scorching hot like an August summer day. The sky was a perfect blue sprinkled with a few cotton-candy like clouds. People were everywhere wandering from stall to stall, buying items from different vendors. In the air was the smell of roasted peanuts, hotdogs and jerk chicken. When Benjamin first saw Winter, she was mulling over a piece of blue and white gingham material, holding up the fabric to her eyes before caressing it with her slender fingers.

Winter was still dancing, and it had left him awkwardly standing there not really doing anything. He began to watch two young children who had moved close to them under the booth to get away from the sun. The chocolate ice cream they were eating dripped over the cones and trickled onto their small fingers. One of the children had devised a plan to lick the runny ice-cream from his hands when the cone wobbled dangerously and overturned onto his shirt. The fright from the mishap rendered him helpless, causing him to freeze in place. The other child believing that the accident was somehow a fault of his own, started to cry loudly. A plump lady with arm rolls, alerted by the sudden howl, came and ushered them off.

"Benjamin! Winter!" The voice was coming from behind the booth.

They turned around to see Oliver, a boy two years older than Benjamin. He had known Oliver since they were toddlers when their parents met at their speech therapy sessions. Benjamin had introduced Oliver to Winter. Oliver wore a cochlear implant for his sensorineural hearing loss. He could not even hear loud sounds without the cochlear implant. Benjamin was born deaf due to congenital abnormalities resulting in his hearing loss, but that was not the case with Oliver. He lost his hearing at age three after he contracted measles. He became profoundly deaf in both ears.

As small children, Oliver and Benjamin attended schools for deaf children where they learnt sign language. They had needs that other children did not have; there were always speech therapy appointments, ears, nose and throat appointments, audiologist appointments, geneticist appointments, and so on. When it was time for high school, Benjamin's mother thought it was best if he attended an inclusive school with regular hearing children. That was where his school journey ended with Oliver who continued in the deaf school. Despite going to different schools, the two boys remained great friends.

"Today is hot," Oliver signed.

"The Caribbean is always hot," Benjamin signed back with a big smile on his face.

Oliver was using a handkerchief to wipe some of the sweat that was rolling down his face.

"Let's get some cold soda from the booth," Benjamin suggested.

Winter was still in a dancing mood but decided to walk with the boys to the booth anyway. She made a remark about the sugar content in soda and got a bottle of water instead; she even insisted that it be spring water. That was another thing about this new Winter, she had suddenly become concerned with petty stuff such as pimples and weight. After they got their beverages, Oliver joined in on Winter's dancing escapade. Benjamin on the other hand was too self-conscious to dance in public.

"Why aren't you dancing Benny?" Winter signed.

"I just don't feel like it," Benjamin signed back.

He did not want his friends to know that he was afraid to let other people see him dance. He spread the towel that he had taken from his backpack onto the soft grass which felt like a cushion when he sat down. He watched as his friends danced but dancing was just not Benjamin's thing; he thought he looked like he was having a seizure even at his least attempt to bust-a-move. He could do simple moves like the dab, but anything more advanced like TikTok dance moves, he would not even attempt. Of course, he attempted them in the privacy of his bedroom, but anywhere outside of that was a big fat no.

At a booth not too far from where the three friends were, people were lined up trying to toss balls into five small buckets which were about twenty feet away. A giant teddy bear was the grand prize for whomever caused the five balls to land inside the buckets without stepping out of the tossing zone. Benjamin sat on his towel, watching several failed attempts to win the bear. He knew that just like in a game of cricket, all it needed was a settled nerve, skill and patience. A chubby girl sucking on a Kisko Pop stepped to the front of the line. She gathered the balls, and before each throw she rubbed the ball between her palms. She threw the first four balls with the ease of an expert, and they landed perfectly inside the buckets. An excited crowd gathered around her and dished out advice in sign language to the girl who was becoming flustered by the attention. She took up the final ball, threw it in the distance and took off running with the kisko pop hanging from her mouth. Benjamin held his head down and laughed at the shocked expressions on the faces of the unwanted advisers.

Oliver tapped Benjamin on his shoulder and signed, "I am starving, let's get lunch before the show starts."

He had stopped dancing and was fumbling around in his pockets for his wallet. Benjamin was happy that they were no longer interested in dancing and wanted to do something else. He folded the towel he was sitting on and shoved it inside his bag. They went to one of the cooked-food vendors and examined the menu and price list taped onto a board at the front of the booth. Benjamin wanted to get the fried fish with bammy, but Winter said there were too many carbohydrates and fats in the foods on the menu. The three friends moved from vendor to vendor, giving Winter the opportunity to examine menus and calculate calories on her smartphone. They walked until they were at the back of the venue, and in the area with the rides.

"Let's get tickets for the rides," Benjamin suggested.

Oliver checked his watch before agreeing that he could only do one ride. The line for the Air-Whizz was short and they got their tickets in no time. Winter was not sure if she wanted to go on the ride with the boys or continue her search for healthy food.

Benjamin convinced her that it would be safe as long as she removed her heavy earrings that could tear her ear lobes with the strong altitude wind.

"Are you sure it's not scary?" she asked nervously for what seemed to be the tenth time.

"It will be fine," Benjamin said, attempting to reassure her about something he had never experienced.

They sat in the first three seats, leaving the fourth seat in the row empty. Winter sat between the boys and removed her earrings. The worker was about to fasten their seat belts when Winter stood up and said that she had changed her mind. It was going to be only Benjamin and Oliver. She took their bags and went to stand at the side of the ticket booth. Benjamin thought he was prepared for what was to come, but the sudden jerk of movement sent his heart plummeting in his chest. Oliver gave out a tiny shriek as they began to rise higher and higher. He could no longer identify Winter on the ground, everyone looked like a tiny speck from the air. There was a sudden whoosh that sent the ride going in every direction. Benjamin looked over at Oliver who had closed his eyes and had his head buried in the back of the chair. He looked as if he was praying. The wind was causing Benjamin's eyes to become watery and the distance from the ground was making him feel lightheaded. The ride went on for what seemed like ages and he had to hold his bladder to prevent himself from wetting his pants. When they got back to the ground, their insides felt jumbled like a puzzle, and their hearts were throbbing like crazy. They both had to stand to the side with their backs bent and their hands resting on their knees, to get their bearings straight.

The lines at the food stalls resembled the many twists and turns of a snake. They seemed to have no end. The stage show would be starting in approximately twelve minutes, and everyone was in a last-minute rush to eat before the performances. Oliver closed his eyes briefly and then opened them as if he was trying to ward off the onset of a headache. Both boys stood in line knowing there would be no time to buy food and then eat before the show. Winter went off to the bathroom and when she came back, Benjamin noticed that she had changed the colour of her lips to a tint of red.

"This won't work," Winter said, pointing to the line. "The poster said that Lila Singh will be here, and I have to get a place at the front."

The food line had barely moved since Winter had left for the bathroom. Led by Oliver, they abandoned the line and eased their way to the front of the eager crowd so that Winter could have a good view of Lila Singh as she had demanded. Two teenage girls were on stage performing a Justin Bieber song; one was singing and the other was signing. The singing girl's voice rolled throughout the venue in splendid waves. A woman went on stage and was using paper money to fan the singing girl's face, like they did at church rallies. The applause was robust when the performers took a bow and exited the stage.

Winter was singing and dancing throughout the stage show, but she became more alive when it was time for the fashion show. She started to shamelessly hop from one foot to the other like a child. Benjamin stared at Winter, not understanding her excitement. In his opinion, the various pieces of clothing by Lila Singh were average looking but most of them were downright zany. The shoulder pads were too pronounced under the thin material of the shirts, and the jackets were too loose on the models.

"I want that dress!" Winter shrieked.

She was pointing at a blue silk dress whose cut Benjamin thought was too fussy for the simplicity of the fabric. He wondered if Winter really loved the designs as much as she was behaving, or if it was pride in knowing that Lila Singh was deaf too. Winter's hopping and screaming was causing him embarrassment. He held his head down, wishing he hadn't got a place at the front. He was shocked. He had never seen Winter behave this excited, especially over crazy-looking clothes.

A short woman emerged on stage wearing a grey ankle length dress, and a black bucket hat with a tape measure draped over her shoulders. Winter was now stomping the ground on her tiptoes, pointing and screaming Lila's name. Lila came to a stop at the front of the stage, waving to the crowd near to where they were standing.

"Reach out and touch the hem of your messiah's garment," Benjamin mocked Winter as she screamed Lila's name. She simply ignored his utterances and continued to scream.

Oliver seemed to be enjoying the show although he was very quiet. He was one of those people who would watch a performance expressionless but could later give every detail. It was a hot day, but by the way he was sweating you would have thought that the sun had made its way to earth and was resting on top of his head. It felt like he had just taken a bath and did not bother to dry himself when he placed his right hand on Benjamin's shoulder.

"Now we have on stage, The Dynamic Dancers!" The announcer was a tall, slim woman wearing a blue bodysuit. Her ribs seemed to be piercing through the fabric every time she spoke. The microphone was attached to her clothes, leaving her hands free to do sign language.

The crowd went wild. The Dynamic Dancers were national champions on the island. Benjamin's neighbour liked to say the name Boneless Bodies would have been a better fit for the group. That was his way of commenting on their insane abilities to contort their bodies. Benjamin looked over at a now calm Winter who was chewing on a piece of gum she had taken from her purse earlier. Oliver's right hand was still on his shoulder but was getting heavier. Benjamin turned to say something to him when it happened.

"Oli-"

In the blink of an eye, his eyes rolled over, his hand slipped off Benjamin's shoulder and Oliver landed on the ground with a loud thud.

CHAPTER

4

The talk of the school was the upcoming musicals that grades seven and eight were going to be hosting. It was like a good neighbourhood gossip; you could not go anywhere without hearing about it. Each grade would be choosing a book or movie to recreate a theatrical type of performance with singing, acting, spoken word and dancing. It was the first time the school was going to be having a musical and all the students were excited. They knew what musicals were, they all had seen *High School Musical* and *Descendants*, or at least Benjamin had seen those. There was so much gossip and talk about everything. During lunch break, Lanay told Benjamin that the grade seven students were going to be doing *The Jungle Book*, although they were still debating about it. After a vote, Benjamin knew for a fact that his grade was going to be doing *Pirates of the Caribbean*.

He met Lanay at the water fountain refilling her bottle after school and she was spitting fire. Her mood seemed to have gone from zero to one hundred in a matter of hours. At lunchtime she was excited about the possibility of her grade doing *The Jungle Book*, but now those plans seemed to have changed permanently, and she was not happy about it. In fact, she was so angry, she could hardly speak clearly.

"That blinking Ms. Ruddoch wants us to do *The Magic School Bus*!" She paused for a moment as if she was letting the words marinate on her tongue.

"Who does she think I am?" She hardly caught her breath before she blurted out, "Not because she looks like Ms. Frizzle, I am not bloody Dorothy Ann!"

Benjamin wanted to laugh because Ms. Ruddoch with her vintage dressing, could have easily passed for the black version of Ms. Frizzle. But given the seriousness of the situation, he kept a straight face.

"It is not so bad Lanay, it could have been *Dora*," Benjamin said.

He was trying desperately to say something to make her feel better, but judging by the look she gave him, he knew that he had failed. She was biting down on her lip as they left the hallway and stepped out in the school yard. She was no longer talking, and he felt desperate to break the silence.

"When does the new season of Angelic Voices begin?" he asked, although he knew it would not be until next year, but he could not think of anything else to say.

"I don't know anything about stupid singing shows," Lanay said, before biting down on her lip again.

When they got to the gate, his mother was already there talking to another parent. Thomas was in his perambulator playing with his squishy toy. He laughed and kicked his chubby legs when he saw Benjamin. Lanay's father's car was parked on the sidewalk, waiting for her. Benjamin bid her farewell, but she barely answered before getting into the backseat. Immediately her mouth began to go a mile a minute. He knew that she was venting to her father as the car drove away. He was tempted to ask his mother for some money to buy custard apples from the cart-vendor, but she had warned him numerous times about buying from the vendors at the gate. Her problem with the vendors did not lay purely on their disregard for the school's no-vending policy, but she was mostly concerned with where they emptied their bladders and where they washed their hands afterwards.

"You look like a dog with two tails," his mother said as they started walking.

Since he was a baby, she had developed the ability to tell his mood through observation.

Norman and his friends were walking behind them, but they dared not lose their places while he was with his mother. They pretended not to notice him.

Benjamin staggered ahead of his mother, impersonating the walk of Captain Jack Sparrow before turning around and telling her about the upcoming musical. She suggested that he audition for the lead role of Captain Jack Sparrow. That role did not interest him, but he did not tell her so. He could not be bothered with her sermon if he should explain why. Who he really wanted to be was Davy Jones; the keeper of the dead man's chest. Secretly, he wanted to be Davy Jones because he was fierce and heartless, sailors everywhere trembled in their boots at the sound of his name. Jack Sparrow was too happy-go-lucky for his liking.

All students were invited to audition for different roles in the show. On the noticeboard was posted the openings for ten main characters to play the roles of Captain Jack Sparrow, Davy Jones, Will Turner, Elizabeth Swann, Hector Barbosa, Tia Dalma, Cutler Beckett, Joshamee Gibbs, James Norrington, and Bootstrap Bill Turner. Interested actors/singers were to be auditioned on Friday in the auditorium. There were to be thirty-two supporting characters playing the roles of Pintell, Ragetti, Cotton, and a host of other sailors and captains. There were other functions such as sound, lighting and make-up that twelve student volunteers were needed for. Maxwell wanted to be the director and Anice wanted to be his assistant.

Everyone was gathered at the noticeboard discussing what role they were interested in playing. Melody with her braggadocious behaviour said her cousin knew Elizabeth Swann in real life and she was going to audition to play her. There were about three boys who wanted to be Captain Jack Sparrow. Willie said he was going to try out for Davy Jones. Benjamin did not think this role would be good for Willie because the role of Davy Jones was a serious one, and Willie was too buffoonish for the position. Benjamin felt confident that he could easily eliminate his competition.

Benjamin's class had science first thing in the morning and Mr. Williams could hardly keep the students in their seats. Their world had become dedicated to the musical. Everyone wanted to know what role the other person was interested in playing. Whenever he was asked, Benjamin lied and said he did not know as yet. He was afraid of the laughter and ridicule that would follow his answer.

"Angella get back to your seat!" Mr. Williams shouted.

She had gotten out of her seat and was walking around with a piece of paper collecting the names and the roles students were interested in playing. Angella was a big girl with a personality of water; it had no shape, colour, or form. She took on the personality of whomever she was with, or whatever was happening around her. She had played a role in all of Benjamin's experiences of bullying. She has been a participant, reinforcer, defender and bystander. He did not care much for her.

They were in the science laboratory conducting an experiment on forces and motion on Earth. Mr. Williams had challenged them to make an empty soda can jump from one mug to another by blowing air. Benjamin was trying to complete the task but the noise in the background made it hard for him to concentrate. He removed his hearing aids briefly because his ears felt like they were about to explode. Mr. Williams was known to be a no-nonsense teacher who was quick to hand out detentions. Even with the possible threat of having to spend their lunch break cleaning beakers and test tubes, there were still loud chatter about the upcoming musical.

The same mood was brought over to the physical education class. The wind was hot on their faces as the boys lined up to race on the freshly marked field. The girls were on the left field in their miniskirts and white tee-shirts with Mrs. Simpson preparing for a game of netball.

"The fastest runner should be Captain Jack Sparrow," Richard said, grinning from ear to ear.

He was the fastest runner in the whole school and he always tried to use running to get his own way. He had won the first and only gold medal for the school at the national championships, an achievement he used to set himself apart from the rest of his grade. Last term he even challenged Mr. Williams to a race for a passing general science grade. The only thing he got from Mr. Williams was a detention.

"You idiot! What does running and acting have in common?" Imran shouted.

Imran was clearly offended. Either he wanted to be Captain Jack Sparrow, or he was tired like the rest of his classmates of Richard using his superior ability to get his own way.

There was roaring laughter at Imran's quick response. When Willie changed his voice to a funny accent to say, "Ahoy mate, I am Captain Jack Sparrow, the sprinter", this made the students laugh even more.

"Boys be quiet!" Mr. Spence shouted. Benjamin had seen him coming from the top of the slope but was not expecting he would have gotten to where they were lining up so quickly. He walked with a permanent uncomfortable gait as if he had done too many squats which had resulted in oversized thighs. The boys did not need to be convinced to close their mouths, none of them wanted to have to drop to the ground and do one hundred push-ups. All throughout the class, the boys made coded comments about Richard and how unreasonable he could be. He did not try to defend himself and pretended as if he was not bothered by their criticism. For the rest of the day, he had earned the nickname 'Ahoy Mate'.

Lunchtime, Lanay met Benjamin at their usual spot. He had chicken patties with homemade carrot juice which Lanay exchanged for her beef lasagna. She was in a much better mood than the one she had left in yesterday. Ms. Ruddoch had reconsidered, and they were going to be performing *The Jungle Book*. Lanay was determined to get the lead role of Mowgli.

"How can you play Mowgli and you are a girl?" Benjamin asked.

"Benjamin Morgan, girls can do anything that boys can do!" she fired back, springing up from the tree and placing her small hands on her waist. He knew that Lanay could be very hardheaded and loved to prove people wrong.

"Why can't you be Kaa?" he asked. Kaa was a girl snake and as far as he was concerned, Kaa would have been a more realistic role for her.

"Because I do not want to be a spineless snake!" she shouted.

He had been in the school long before she was, and he knew that there was no way she was going to get the role of Mowgli. The principle of the school was that only boys should get boy roles and girls should get girl roles. Right there and then, he knew that he should prepare himself for the day when a disappointed Lanay would return to him upset because she did not get to be Mowgli.

Taken aback by her growing anger, he asked "Why are you being so hostile?"

She hissed through her teeth, narrowed her eyes and said, "I am not hostile, I am passionate. It would serve you to learn the difference."

Realizing there was going to be no chance of him convincing passionate Lanay to audition for a more realistic role, he ate the cold lasagna in silence. A very uncomfortable silence.

For the rest of the week, Lanay ignored him and he did not try to speak to her either. He did not want to seem pitiful sitting under the tree by himself so every lunchtime, he brought a book and pretended that he was busy reading or doing a puzzle. He even got Mr. Lewis to join him a few days. Lanay started to hang with the self-proclaimed cool kids. Benjamin thought they were nitwits who wanted to be cool so badly that they named themselves 'Cool Kids'. Whenever she saw him walking by, she would immediately be bent over in laughter, pretending that something one of her new friends had said was suddenly hilarious. She had begun to wear her socks unfolded, pulled up to her calves just like the other girls in the group. Benjamin consoled himself by thinking that Lanay had lost her mirror along with her senses, because her stubby legs covered with long socks made her look like a basic school child. He told himself that he did not need Lanay anyway, he did not associate with traitors. It was not as if he could not make friends, he chose not to make friends.

Every night after he was done with his homework, Benjamin would transform into Davy Jones. He breathed his air. He spoke his language. He even borrowed one of his mother's wigs and pretended that it was tentacles hanging from his face. The students had been given a direct quote from Davy Jones to practice for the audition, and Benjamin rehearsed it until he began to sound like a broken record.

"Dead men tell no tales…
Ah, but they do tell tales. So says I, Davy Jones
Dead men tell no tales
If ye be brave or fool enough to face a pirate's curse, proceed.
Dead men tell no tales…
Ha! Ha! Ha! Ha! Ha! Ha!"

His father was not away auditing, and so he helped Benjamin until he got the lines perfectly. All throughout the week he was singing and practicing Davy Jones impressions. He even watched the movie again. Not to seem conceited, but he was impressed with himself. He had become better at being Davy Jones than Davy Jones himself.

Friday came and Benjamin was sweating bullets. It had come down to the moment of truth and he did not know what to do with himself. All throughout the day, the different classes filed in and out of the auditorium. The audition panel was made up of the performing arts teacher - Mrs. Kennedy, Mr. Gowe - the art teacher, and Mrs. Prescott – the music teacher. Benjamin's fight for the role was not going to be as easy as he had earlier speculated. Along with Willie, there were two other boys who were also trying out for the role of Davy Jones. He felt threatened and started to doubt himself.

The students were handed numbers and were told to wait until they heard their number called to go on stage. Benjamin was going to be candidate number three. Candidate number one spoke with a lisp and he was even more nervous than Benjamin. He kept on forgetting his lines and it was obvious that Mrs. Kennedy was becoming impatient with him. She would pull her glasses to the tip of her nose and level a piercing gaze at the stage. Benjamin felt reassured that he was not going to be a threat to him, who was more Davy Jones than Davy Jones himself. Candidate number two was a tall, lanky boy who went by the name of Patrick. He was a part of the school's quiz team and was popular with the teachers. Patrick was a perfectionist, and his command of the stage would have anyone believing he was professionally trained at the Edna Manley College of the Visual and Performing Arts. All the reasons for Benjamin to run from the auditorium filled his mind. In his head, he knew that Patrick was going to be his biggest competition.

Benjamin felt the pressure from Patrick's A-list performance when his number was called. He felt a mild panic as he walked towards the stage. He had excessively big shoes to fill. He stepped onstage, raised his head, and pushed his shoulders back.

"Dead men tell no tales," Benjamin began. He was speaking as slowly and clearly as he could.

After each line, he took a short pause to emphasize the confidence in his speaking and pronounce the words he struggled with saying. The brightness of his voice rolled off his tongue and into the audience. His father had given him that tip and had told him to maintain eye contact with the panel. Benjamin tried to follow this advice but, in that moment, he saw no one and he heard no one. It was only Davy Jones on the stage. The end of his performance was met with pockets of applause, which made him both happy and scared. He was not sure if they were clapping because they were impressed with his performance or if he had done so poorly, they were happy to see him go.

At the last minute, Willie opted out of the audition. He had mistakenly practiced for the role of Davy Jones, the British singer from the band The Monkees. That was the nature of Willie, he never took anything seriously and never seemed to be bothered by anything.

CHAPTER

5

t was hard for Lanay to keep up appearances with the Cool Kids and very soon she came crawling back to Benjamin like a prodigal child begging for forgiveness. Okay, that was not exactly how it happened. She casually met him at the staircase landing and started talking like nothing had happened.

"What are you doing after school Benny?" she asked.

He was not in the mood to talk to her about after school plans. He held his face somber-like, not wanting to give her the idea that all was well between them. He wanted to denounce her for being a sell-out. He wanted to shun her for turning her back on him because she could not handle the truth.

"I will be going home; I have swim practice this afternoon," Benjamin responded.

He knew what she really wanted to ask, but she was afraid to. She had made it bad enough to be hanging with the Cool Kids. Lanay could not risk being further judged as being shallow by asking about an unimportant party invitation.

Apart from the musical, Jordan's upcoming birthday party was on everybody's lips. Jordan was believed to be the richest boy in the school. His father drove a very nice car and rumour had it that his house looked like Buckingham Palace. He had announced that the invitations to his party would be handed out after school that day. Benjamin was not one who cared for elaborate nonsense like birthday party invitations, but he was interested to see the extravagant way it would be done. Everyone knew that nothing with Jordan was ever normal. He did not want Lanay to know that he was interested though. He did not want to seem desperate and foolish to want to see an invitation.

"Are you going to wait for the invitations?" Lanay asked.

"If you want to." Benjamin shrugged his shoulders, pretending not to care.

There was a huge gathering at the gate eagerly awaiting the invitations Jordan would come bearing. Lanay and Benjamin were right there in the thick of things, standing with their backs leaned against the wall, partially covering the metal carving with the school's name. It was not their practice to hang around after school, but they could not miss this for the world. Benjamin's mother was chatting with her friend and had agreed to wait for a few minutes. They did not have to wait for long. Jordan's father drove up in a brown topless car with a man dressed as a butler from the olden Victorian Era days to hand out the party invitations. Jordan was doing a little dance, relishing the spotlight. The butler stepped out of the car and removed the steel cloche from the platter he was holding in his hand like he was about to serve food to guests at a dinner party. Piles of envelopes were revealed. Jordan looked about the crowd like a king addressing his lowly subjects.

"Alright everyone, if you want to come to my party, just come and get an invitation. I have eighty of them," he said.

There was a mad rush of students scrambling everywhere to get one of the desired invitations. Without care for appearances, Lanay swooped through the crowd like an eagle and returned waving two envelopes bounded by gold glitter. Her uniform was rumpled, and a ribbon was missing from her loose ponytail, but she could not have cared less.

"Benny! These are for us!" she screamed excitedly.

He took the envelope and tried to appear as unexcited as he could. Inside was a picture of Jordan dressed in a gold jacket, white pants and white sneakers. His waist length locks hung loosely and added to the iconic look of the photo. On the picture were the words 'Party with the Prince' in bright, gold writing. Benjamin was excited. What was happening to him seemed to be happening to everyone else around him; they were all excited, but the other students were not afraid to let it show. As excited as he was, Benjamin believed that the party was not going to be a place for him. Moreover, no one from school had ever invited him to their birthday party.

"Give this to someone else." He was attempting to put the invitation back into Lanay's hands. She rejected it by shaking her head from side to side and holding her hands behind her back.

"You have to take it back. I won't be going," Benjamin said.

She stared at him piercingly before walking away. He started walking briskly behind her, waving the invitation in the air, trying to get her attention. He tried to pull the back of her tunic to drop the envelope in the gap between her tunic and white blouse, but she turned around and smacked his hand.

"Benjamin Morgan, if you come even an inch closer, I am going to knock you out. You will be going and that's that." She flounced to the waiting car, turning around just long enough to give him a threatening look before getting in and slamming the door.

Benjamin opened his mathematics book and placed the invitation between its pages. His mother had noticed the exchange between him and Lanay and wanted to know what happened. He explained that Lanay was forcing him to attend the party, but he could not give his mother a good reason why he did not want to go. His mother agreed with Lanay since he did not have an excuse. Not that he was surprised that his mother agreed with Lanay, he thought that girls always agreed with each other. No one had ever invited him to a birthday party, and he did not want to go somewhere he was not going to be welcomed.

"Benny you have to come out of your shell," his mother said, rubbing his coily hair and kissing his forehead. Little else was said between them on the walk home. The only other time his mother spoke was when she handed him the stroller and went to break a few stalks of mint that were growing wildly on a little hill, not far from the roadway.

For four days, Benjamin could think of nothing else. The party was going to be that Saturday and he had so many decisions to make. He was not sure what he would be wearing. He was not sure if he would feel left out. He was not sure if he could cope with the noisy environment. He just was not sure if he really wanted to go. But having a ticket to Jordan's party was like having a golden ticket to teen heaven. He would be crazy to miss it. Plus, Lanay would never forgive him after she had risked her life to get the invitations, as she reminded him all week at school.

The week went by in a hurry. He had made up his mind to attend the party, since it seemed as if he had no other option. The more he thought about it, the more he thought that maybe it was time for him to get out of his shell, after all, Paul Dore did not get to be Paul Dore by staying in his shell. He went to his mother asking for her fashion advice on what he should wear to the party. She was with Thomas in the living room who was kicking his legs in his highchair and rocking his body every time Deniece Williams' voice came over the CD player singing *Let's Hear it for the Boy*. Having the old CD player in the living room was something that caused him embarrassment whenever guests came over, but his mother used the opportunity to boast that she had had it since her university days.

"Come and dance with us!" his mother shouted above the music.

She held his hands and pulled him forward. She was rocking her body and he followed her steps shyly. This was going to be his first opportunity to attend a real birthday party and he wanted to make an impression. His mother ignored his question about what he should wear as she belted out, "Let's give the boy a hand." He asked the question again, but her only reaction was her twinkling eyes as she sang louder while moving her body mechanically like a robot. It was obvious that she did not have any fashion advice to give so he went and sat in the sofa, watching his mother and little brother dancing. As thoughts of the well-dressed Benjamin he wanted to be at the party played on his mind, he remembered that Winter and Oliver were waiting for him.

He leapt out of the sofa, leaving his mother and Thomas dancing, and ran to his bedroom for his cellphone that was laying on the bed. The screen showed three missed calls from Winter and Oliver. He had forgotten about their video call, although it was something they did every Saturday morning at the same time. Jordan's birthday party had filled his mind and made him forget about his friends.

Oliver and Winter were already deep in conversation when he joined the chat. The two were having a conversation about why some people with hearing loss preferred to be referred to as deaf, some as being hearing impaired and others as being hard-of-hearing. Benjamin hated when he was called hearing impaired because it made him feel like he was improperly made. He remained silent and then he spoke.

"Sorry for being late but my pet lizard ate my cellphone," he signed.

That was his best attempt at a joke to apologize for his tardiness. It seemed to have worked because Winter was immediately bent over in laughter. In her arms she had a black and white dog that was wearing a pink collar with the name Paris written on it in sparkly letters. The dog was not as small as he had expected, but it was still a small dog with a compactly built body.

The joke about the lizard eating the phone had not gone over Oliver's head, and he too was laughing. Benjamin was not expecting this immediate reaction from him because Oliver was one of those people who would get a joke late and laugh long after it had been forgotten. His jawline seemed a little more chiseled than usual, but other than that, he looked well. Their parents had spoken but Benjamin had not seen or spoken to him since the Deaf Retreat where he fainted. Since the incident, Winter had been having a ball mocking Benjamin's frightened reaction to Oliver fainting. She would place both hands on her head and scream, "We need an ambulance!" before collapsing in laughter. But Benjamin was terrified when he saw Oliver on the ground; he thought Oliver was dead. He even had visions in his head of him calling Oliver's mother and delivering the devastating news to her that her only child had died. Winter said that her mocking Benjamin was revenge for him joking about her name.

"How are you managing with everything, Oliver?" Benjamin had a look of empathy on his face. For some reason he was expecting Oliver's eyes to well up with tears and for him to cry about how unfair life was to him.

"I am coping well with my Double D's," Oliver signed back.

He used his hands to make the outline of a woman's chest before laughing loudly. Benjamin did not know how Oliver could joke about something so serious. He only had Norman to deal with and it was causing him multiple sleepless nights. Benjamin would have been overwhelmed with being deaf and also being diabetic. Oliver's fainting spell was because of his blood sugar getting too low since they had skipped lunch at the retreat.

Winter had worked as a filing clerk at a health center last summer and because of this, she felt knowledgeable about all ailments. "Are you on insulin?" she asked Oliver.

Before she could get into Dr. Winter mode, Benjamin changed the subject. Last week she had given him a long lecture about increasing his Vitamin C intake, just because he had coughed once. He was not in the mood to hear another lecture from Winter, even if it was not directed at him.

"Will you guys be going to camp this summer?" Benjamin signed.

Winter gave a soft hiss, rolled her full eyes, and began to go off in sign language.

"My drill instructors don't think it would be a good idea," she said.

Whenever she was upset, she referred to her parents as drill instructors. The use of sign language was also to hide what she was saying, since she was the only one in her household who spoke the language. Benjamin did the same thing sometimes with his parents too, although his mother knew how to sign a few basic words.

None of the three friends had ever been to summer camp although they really wanted to go. It seemed a little suspicious to them that all three parents had said the same thing when they were asked. They said that the risk of mishaps for deaf children were far greater than for normal hearing children. This reason seemed a bit hypocritical to Benjamin because his parents would scold him whenever he tried to use his hearing loss as an excuse. Last month, he decided not to join the youth choir performance at church because the background noise was going to be too much with the drumming, singing and shouts of hallelujah. His mother told him off and reminded him that the Bible said, "To whom much is given, much is expected." He could not understand why his parents were now using his deafness as a reason not to send him to camp.

Oliver said he would be going to America to visit his aunt, and maybe they would go to Disney World.

Lucky guy, Benjamin thought to himself.

Benjamin wanted to confide in his two friends about the troubles he was having with Norman at school. Since the auditorium incident, Norman had seen him many times, but he had not been able to inflict any further damage to him. Norman had this terrifying presence which could be felt almost everywhere in the school, and Benjamin could feel his eyes piercing the back of his head over and over again. They all knew it; no one disrespected Norman and got away with it. Up until now, Benjamin had been kept safe by the protective view of the teachers, hall monitors and safety guards cleverly placed all over the school to monitor students' comings and goings. But he knew that his time was coming, and it was coming up fast.

Benjamin did not want to change the mood of the conversation, so he kept his problems to himself. In his mind, he knew that he had to put an end to Norman's reign of terror once and for all. But he would have to come up with that plan at another time; today was all about Jordan's party.

He did not stay on the call for much longer. Benjamin always loved talking with Winter and Oliver, but he needed to continue his mission to find nice clothes to wear to the party. He had a lot of hard choices to make; he could not decide if he should wear a tee-shirt or a button-down shirt. He could not decide between his tennis sneakers or his Timberlands. It was an even harder decision if he should wear a hat and sunglasses. In the end, he decided to wear a checkered shirt with a pair of dark blue jeans. The Timberlands went better with the outfit. His mother said he looked as if he was on the way to rob a bank with the hat and sunglasses, so he ditched both.

Entering through the huge iron gates of Jordan's house was like entering a royal mansion. Along the brightly lit driveway, the lawn grass shone like an emerald. The house itself was a mini version of Buckingham Palace. Benjamin had never been to Buckingham Palace, but he had seen it enough times on television to imagine what the inside looked like. From the high ceilings hung huge, sparkly chandeliers. The walls were decorated with bold paintings, each with a unique story. It was obvious that it was the house of wealthy people. As the students arrived, they showed their invitations and were led down a wide staircase with oak banisters to the basement where loud music, party lights and peals of laughter echoed throughout the large room which was almost as big as Benjamin's house. He was astonished; he did not know that there were houses in Jamaica that had basements.

A tall woman who Benjamin assumed to be Jordan's mother, was at the base of the stairs handing out party favours containing castle keychains, gold crown picture frames and personalized phone ring holders. Benjamin was especially happy to be getting the phone ring holder which he could use to balance his phone on any flat surface, leaving his hands free to do sign language with Winter and Oliver.

"Are you having a good time?" the tall woman asked. Benjamin had to read her lips because of the loud music in the background.

"Yes ma'am." He nodded as he took the small bag with the party items from her hand.

The party was already in full swing and Benjamin quickly scanned the room, trying to find Lanay. Men dressed smartly as butlers were walking around with trays of juices, saltfish fritters, jerked sausages and chicken kebabs. There was a section which resembled a fast-food restaurant where party attendants were getting burgers and sodas. There was another section for people who only ate seafood and vegetables. It seemed as if the whole school was there, even Norman who still had a score to settle with Benjamin. He made his way past Norman and went to the area with the fast food. Norman's presence at the party was not a threat to Benjamin, as a matter of fact, he was the least of Norman's concern. Norman's head was still wrapped in plastic bandages from the injury he had received at Thursday's match. He was a part of the school's wrestling team and had accidently received a knee to his head while trying to takedown his opponent. The physical injury was minor, but it had resulted in what the principal had told the students was called hyposmia. Benjamin later found out that this was a reduction in Norman's ability to detect odors. Norman always looked messy at school, but even at the party he looked sloppy in an oversized white shirt and a pair of distressed jeans.

Benjamin wandered around looking at the other teenagers who were dancing, eating, talking, laughing and having a good time. Jordan had not yet made his royal entry and he still had not seen Lanay either. It was getting late and she was nowhere to be found. Imran approached him with his mouth filled with fried chicken and chips; small lines of sweat were trickling down his flat copper-colored face. Benjamin thought that he looked out of place in a burgundy jodhpuri suit which would have been better suited for a traditional Indian wedding.

"Have you heard that an entertainer will be here?" Imran asked.

Benjamin could not hear his voice over the loud music and

had to depend on lip reading. "I guess it will be someone big," he responded to Imran.

"I know exactly who is coming but I have sworn to keep it a secret," replied a grinning Imran.

In the back of Benjamin's head, he knew that Imran was lying. Imran was always lying. Benjamin decided he would not give him the satisfaction he desired. He decided not to beg Imran to reveal the great secret to him. Benjamin shrugged his shoulders, pretending that he did not care to know. Imran stood in front of Benjamin, still grinning. After a few seconds, he realized that Benjamin was unwilling to participate in his nonsense and walked away. Benjamin continued eating his cheeseburger but still felt a little disappointed that he could not find Lanay. Benjamin had requested habanero peppers on his burger since the name sounded foreign and he had never had it before. The peppers scorched his tongue, and he had to drink down many glasses of juice to bring relief to it.

Jordan came in on a golden chariot carried by six men dressed as royal guards. His locks were tied with gold chords over which a golden crown hung unsteadily. He looked sharp in a black suit with a pair of low ivory sneakers. For most of the night, he mingled with the crowd with the ease and grace of a superstar. There was a professional photographer capturing memories of the unforgettable night. A large, bejeweled golden chair was placed in front of a golden backdrop which served as the photo area. Students were lined up to have their pictures taken by the photographer. The line was long, but the music and the vibe of the party made up for the wait. Benjamin was almost at the front of the line when a voice came delicately over the microphone.

"It is that time of the night everyone!"

The room went quiet as their attention went to the stage. The woman who Benjamin assumed to be Jordan's mother had the microphone at her mouth.

"Prince Jordan please come to the stage." Her voice was so gentle it caused Benjamin to wonder if it was her everyday voice.

She repeated the request, using one hand to hold the microphone and the other to fidget with the necklace around her neck.

The golden curtains that were drawn since the start of the party, were pulled back to reveal a table with the biggest cake Benjamin had ever seen. It was a stunning three-tier cake; the bottom and top tiers were a beautiful pearl white colour, and the middle tier was of a shimmery gold to match the golden crown serving as the topper. Jordan appeared from the awe-struck crowd to join his mother on stage.

It was time to cut the cake. The deejay played the birthday song and the party guests all sang along to wish Jordan a happy birthday. There were hooting and clapping as he took the cake knife and made two gentle cuts to reveal a slice of creamy red velvet cake. Jordan beamed with pride as his mother hugged him.

"Jordan is so lucky!" Benjamin did not look to see who he was talking to, but from the corner of his eye he saw the person nodding in agreement.

The mood of the party made him forget about the absence of Lanay, and all he wanted to do was dance. He took a chicken kebab on a skewer and a cup of soda from the tray of one of the servers who were still making their way through the crowd. Benjamin was shy at first, but he could not help rocking his head and shoulders to the music, and slowly his whole body became involved in the movement. He felt good sipping on his soda and sliding chunks of chicken into his mouth while he danced.

Benjamin ate and danced until the midnight alarm went off on his phone in his pocket. He had agreed to meet his father out front at midnight. He found Jordan's mother and told her that his father was waiting for him on the outside. She followed him to the door and watched as he got into the waiting vehicle. As the car drove off, heavy raindrops came tumbling from the skies. He'd had such a good time; he could not believe that Lanay had missed out on the party of the century.

CHAPTER

6

The family was up unusually early for a Sunday morning. Benjamin still had not recovered fully from Jordan's birthday party and his eyes felt heavy. He sat on his bed and shuddered at the memory of how shamelessly he had allowed himself to dance at the party, and wished he could take it back. He hoped at least that no one had noticed him dancing and would make fun of him at school for it. His father was giving Thomas a bath and he was splish-splashing soapy water and making a mess in the bathroom. His mother was busying herself in the kitchen with hominy corn porridge and boiled eggs for breakfast. Benjamin's family was getting ready to go to St. Ann to celebrate the 50th wedding anniversary of his grandparents.

Benjamin was extremely excited, his three cousins who lived in America were going to be there. His Uncle George and Aunt Nina were also going to be there. Aunt Nina was a university professor in America, Uncle George on the other hand was a rather mysterious man. He was always busy. Whenever Benjamin visited, Uncle George would pop his head from his bedroom–office for a few minutes to exchange greetings and then he would disappear again. Years ago, he promised Benjamin to one day play cricket with him, but he still had not gotten around to doing so. Benjamin often imagined that his uncle was working on a time-altering invention when he was locked away in his bedroom-office for hours.

The ride to St. Ann was an uneventful one. Thomas was in his car seat sedated by the Tylenol drops he had been given to relieve his teething pain. He slept throughout most of the journey. Benjamin's parents were singing along with the songs that were coming through the car radio. He had downloaded a whole playlist of songs on Spotify for them to choose from, but they kept on going back to the same three songs repeatedly.

The bumps in the road and the repeated songs made him sluggish and he fell asleep. When he woke up, they were in Ocho Rios driving past the one-legged coconut vendor who had a small group of tourists gathered at his stall at the side of the road. Their faces showed amusement, as the vendor wielded his glistening machete and made expert chops in the jelly coconuts he was selling to them. The car radio was off, and Benjamin rolled his window down to listen to the sound of the waves that were crashing against the shore as they drove along the beautiful countryside. There was just something about listening to waves that made Benjamin happy. Maybe it was because his hearing loss meant that his ears could not receive sound waves without his hearing aids, so he appreciated hearing the waves of the sea.

His grandmother was working in her flower garden when they arrived. The hibiscus hedges looked as if they were being maintained by a mathematician; not one flower was out of place. The daisies, butterfly jasmines, blooming dahlias and orchids, each had their rightful place in the well-maintained garden. Benjamin thought that his grandmother had every right to be as proud as she was of her garden. She had spent endless hours pruning and watering the plants, and her labor had not been in vain. The yard looked like it was a picture taken from a Swiss postcard.

"My boy you are almost as big as your daddy now," his grand-mother said, while staring at him from his head to toe.

His grandmother chose to call him 'my boy' rather than just simply saying Benny like everyone else. Before he could respond, she gave him an enormous hug which made his hearing aids squeak and left him gasping for air.

"Hey mamaw," he responded when he regained his composure.

Benjamin's grandmother was in a white jumpsuit with a belt around her waist. She always wore white; be it funeral, wedding, graduation, gardening, no matter the occasion, everyone knew that she was going to be wearing white. Benjamin quietly examined his grandmother and wondered how come she never got dirt on her clothes even when she was gardening. He was sure she would have a panic attack if a speck of dirt should accidently land on her.

"Ho ho ho! I thought I heard voices." Benjamin's grandfather laughed as he emerged from the house dressed in a white linen shirt, which Benjamin assumed was chosen by his grandmother. His shirt was coordinated with grey linen pants.

"Benny has Jennifer been feeding you fertilizer?" his grandfather asked as soon as he saw him.

Benjamin's mother chuckled proudly at his grandfather's question. He did not wait for a response from Benjamin and Benjamin was happy because he was not sure what to say. His grandfather rubbed his head then reached over to take Thomas from his mother's arms. Thomas was rubbing his gum against his teething ring and was releasing long drools of water over his grandfather's arms. Benjamin found this funny.

"Nina is on her way with the kids," Benjamin's grandfather said while looking at his father.

Aunt Nina had left earlier with her children to go for a morning dip at Ocho Rios Bay Beach. Her three children were Kyle who was 18, Jaden who was 14, and baby Zoey who was two. As usual, Uncle George was being busy in his room and had not yet thought of the visitors as being worthy of his greetings.

Inside the house was spotless. They all knew the rules; outdoor shoes were totally forbidden inside the house. There were to be absolutely no running either. His grandmother would rather lose a leg than to get dirt on her expensive rug. Benjamin thought that his grandparent's house was like a museum for expensive artifacts from all over the world. The Persian rug in the living-room was handmade and was of pure silk. There were Chinese porcelain, German pottery, African masks and statues, Haitian paintings, Venetian pieces, Bohemian crystal, among other fragile fangles and dangles. The cleaning lady smiled at them when they walked in. She had just removed some washed clothes from the line at the back of the yard and was transporting them in a wicker basket to the guest room. Benjamin's grandmother told her that she could leave the ironing until she returned on Monday. She pretended to protest the decision, but Benjamin had sensed the joy in her eyes. His grandmother got a purse from her handbag and handed the cleaning lady a few crumpled notes.

They all sat at the kitchen island and grandma offered them a platter with fruits. Benjamin had never seen anyone eat fruits with a knife and fork, but that was how his grandma was having the diced pineapples on her plate. He had seen her eat her fruits like that numerous times before, but the degree of his surprise always remained the same. She was chewing slowly as if she was counting each bite. The cleaning lady, now wearing a denim dress and a wig, poked her head through the kitchen door and told everyone goodbye.

"Mamaw may I have something to drink?" Benjamin asked.

He really wanted to ask for soda, but he already knew the answer. She gave him a glass of chilled almond milk which he drank down in big gulps. His grandmother was as committed to her health as she was to her garden. Thomas had started to fuss when Aunt Nina walked in with Benjamin's three cousins. She had an air of confidence about her, you just had to know that she was present. She was a small woman who wore her natural hair in a wavy twist-out pattern. Despite her mother's no shoe in the house rule, on her feet she wore flat, leather sandals. She was one of those people who seemed to be permanently smiling.

"Look at you Lennox! What is that I see, a gut?" she asked sarcastically, patting Benjamin's father's rounded belly.

"It is almost as big as yours," his father responded jokingly.

With that, Aunt Nina folded her fists and pretended that she was going to knock him for six. Benjamin's father pretended to dodge her punch and the two hugged and began to giggle like playful children. They all laughed.

Kyle, Jaden and Benjamin quietly slipped away to get down to their own mischief as the adults became consumed in a heated debate over international politics. Benjamin had not seen his cousins in a long time and he was fascinated by them, especially Jaden. Jaden had a way of speaking and ending every sentence with 'ya know', even when he was not expecting an answer. It was not really a question, it was just something that he said. Benjamin thought that maybe it was the American way of speaking, but it seemed cool. There was not much to do in the yard and Kyle wanted to watch basketball on television; the sport never interested Benjamin. He thought of it as being the male version of netball and netball was for girls. He preferred the more rugged game of cricket because it took real muscles and strategy to hold a bat and swing it precisely to hit a ball over the boundary.

With Kyle gone, Jaden and Benjamin sat on chairs in the garden, calculating their next move. Jaden fetched two bars of Snickers from his pocket which both boys ate cautiously to avoid bits of chocolate and peanuts from smearing their faces and clothes. They were trying to avoid their grandmother's reprimand and lecture about childhood diabetes.

"Have you seen Uncle George as yet?"

Benjamin could not resist, he had to ask as inappropriate as it may have seemed.

"I saw him two nights ago getting a drink from the refrigerator, ya know," Jaden said. They both went silent and after a few minutes Jaden said, "Mom says he has always been nocturnal, ya know."

Jaden must have realized that Benjamin was baffled by the mystery they called Uncle George and he sought to provide some understanding.

In Benjamin's mind, Uncle George was just like a reclusive hermit who ate cats and only went outside when no one was looking. The boys soon forgot about Uncle George and started talking about their gaming consoles. Benjamin had received a PlayStation 4 last year as a Christmas gift from his maternal grandparents but now he wanted a PlayStation 5. Jaden was telling him how lucky he was because he still had a PlayStation 3, but he was hoping to get an upgraded one for his birthday.

The scent coming from the kitchen was making their stomachs growl. The light grey smoke from the jerk pan floated off in the mid-afternoon sky. The adults were busy preparing the food. Aunt Nina called out to Kyle to come and help with chopping the fruits to make a juice cocktail to go with the dinner. The yard had a festive scent of bold, vibrant Caribbean spices which was making the boys hungry. They had heard a shuffle in Uncle George's bedroom-office about thirty minutes earlier, but he still had not emerged from his domain. They got tired of waiting to see him.

"Let's go to the pond," Benjamin suggested. He had gotten up off the bench and was standing on his tiptoes while extending his arms over his head.

Benjamin was warned numerous times not to go to the pond, but he had nothing better to do. Plus, if they were caught and was being scolded, he could always say that the smoke from the jerk pan was affecting his ears, that was why he left the yard. His Ears Nose and Throat (ENT) Specialist always reminded him to stay away from any environment with a lot of dust and smoke. Jaden agreed and they slipped through the gate before any of the adults noticed. They believed that it made no sense to seek permission to do something they knew was forbidden.

There was nothing much to see at the pond. The only bit of entertainment were the striking cymbals and singing coming from the Baptist church across the road. Benjamin's only reason for suggesting that they go to the pond was because he was warned to stay away from the pond and was curious to see it. Jaden picked up a small stone and threw it towards the water. It made three little circles before disappearing in the murky, still pond. Benjamin was not to be outdone and picked up a stone and threw it in the water in a similar fashion. His stone immediately sank without making any circles. The following two stones he threw embarrassed him in the same manner, but he tried until he was making three and four circles. For the rest of the time at the pond, Benjamin and Jaden were involved in a secret competition of stone throwing although neither of them verbalized it.

The boys quietly slipped back into the yard, hoping that their absence was not noticed. The smell of curry greeted their nostrils as they crouched to close the gate behind them. They sat out front and knocked their shoes against a large stone in the yard to remove the wet clay that was clinging to the bottoms. For a few minutes they lingered in the yard, examining the funny-looking gnomes that were the latest addition to their grandmother's garden. Not too long after, they decided to go inside to see what everyone else was doing. Benjamin's mother and Aunt Nina were setting the table in the dining room. This was quite unusual, as their grandmother only allowed the use of the dining room for special occasions. She had even brought out some of her expensive porcelain dinnerware which she bragged about receiving as a wedding gift fifty years ago. Their grandmother offered the boys baby carrots as they passed through the kitchen to get to the backyard where Benjamin's father and grandfather were putting the last touches on the jerk meat.

Kyle was standing between the two men, pretending to be interested in the conversation that was going on. He stood with his right leg bent at the knee, in front of the left one, while holding a bottle of water. He nodded as the men spoke and could have easily been mistaken for a bright, college student immersed in a lecture. The two men still had not agreed to disagree over the debate they were having earlier.

In the corner of Benjamin's eyes, he saw his Uncle George seated on an iron chair leaning against the wall. Benjamin did not want to stare but even the facial expression that Uncle George held was one of mystery. He could not tell if he was genuinely interested in the conversation, or if he was there because he felt he had to be there. Uncle George was Benjamin's grandparent's last child. He was in his late thirties, but it was hard to tell his real age because he had this boyish incompleteness about him. He was dressed in blue denim pants, blue polo shirt and blue Nikes. That was another thing that Benjamin noticed about Uncle George, he did not like to mix colors and always wore the same colors throughout. Uncle George smiled at him in acknowledgement, and he smiled back. Benjamin was tempted to ask him what he spent his time doing in his bedroom-office, but he knew that his mother would probably skin him alive if he did.

It was almost 3 p.m. and the adults were in a hurry to make the final touches to dinner. Jaden went inside to help his mother with the vegetables. Uncle George and Benjamin were left in the backyard staring at each other. Uncle George eventually spoke but he did not make mention of the cricket game, and Benjamin did not mention it either. He did not mention what he spent time doing in his bedroom-office and Benjamin did not mention it either. They spoke about other things, more important things like Norman. For some reason, Benjamin trusted Uncle George to give him this information about his school life. As odd as he was, Uncle George always made him feel special, although Benjamin believed it was his hearing situation which made Uncle George have pity on him. He was the only person in the whole family who could expect a Christmas gift from Uncle George every year. Last year he sent him a box of silk handkerchiefs.

"Mrs. Morgan." There was a brief pause and then the call came again from the front yard.

Benjamin's grandmother left what she was doing in the kitchen and shortly returned with a lady dressed in church attire. She was wearing one of those wide-brimmed hats that blocked the view of everyone sitting in the pews behind her. Benjamin had seen the woman before, he remembered her holding down the hem of his mother's white dress as she was being immersed in the baptismal pool at his grandmother's church. Benjamin had been introduced to her on that occasion, but his grandmother always relished in the opportunity to introduce him to her friends.

There was a polite smile on their grandmother's face as she introduced her grandchildren to her friend Mrs. Pearle. "These two young men are my grandsons Jaden and My Boy Benjamin." Their grandmother rubbed their faces with her oily fingers resting into their skin.

Mrs. Pearle narrowed her eyes and took a closer look at the two boys. "These are the two boys I saw earlier throwing stones at the crocodiles in the pond," she said, still examining their faces.

The colour left their faces and they uneasily stood there, not knowing what to do with themselves. All eyes were focused on them and they did not know what to say.

"We… we… we," Benjamin stammered, but nothing else left his lips.

He wanted to say they had not left the yard, but he feared his lie being discovered and being ordered on his knees by his grandmother to ask God for forgiveness and control over his lying lips.

"They were with me," Uncle George said. "I brought them to the pond but left them out front and came inside."

Benjamin allowed himself to breathe a sigh of relief. Uncle George hardly spoke, so it was easy for the adults to believe whatever he said. Him making an excuse for them eased the dryness in Benjamin's throat. He looked at Uncle George and smiled as a rush of joy overtook his body.

"Umph," said a sighing Mrs. Pearle. The mole on her top lip shook as she continued to examine their faces. She did not say anything else, except to bid them farewell and left with her King James Bible tucked beneath her arm.

That was not the only surprise Uncle George had for his family that day. Benjamin saw a different side of him at the dinner table. He had been behaving strangely all afternoon; smiling and being helpful. Benjamin was in between big bites of fried chicken when Uncle George stood and proposed to give a toast. Everyone was focused on him, so Benjamin used the opportunity to lick the chicken grease from his fingers without being admonished by his mother or grandmother for behaving like a pig at the table.

The toast was dedicated to his parents and he spoke slowly with a lisp. "I want us all to raise our glasses to the backbone of our family. May you both have many more years ahead of health, joy, and happiness. Because of you, we are."

No one expected this from Uncle George. Benjamin started shuffling the napkin holder at the center of the table to distract himself from the discomfort he felt as his uncle spoke. Benjamin could hardly believe that this was the same Uncle George who would merely stick his head out to say hello before going back in to hiding, but he was now acting as the master of ceremonies.

What has the world come to? Benjamin thought.

Benjamin's grandfather pursed his lips and did not say anything, but his grandmother began to sob lightly. Aunt Nina patted her mother's back lightly like old people do at funerals. Their spectacle was not having a lasting effect on Benjamin's appetite. The food was delicious and he hungrily poked big spoonfuls of rice and peas in his mouth. Even the fruit cocktail that Kyle had helped with was refreshing; it had the right amounts of fruits, ginger and lime. Benjamin was happy. Sitting at the table with his family made him realize that we all were special to someone.

CHAPTER

7

Since his auditorium altercation with Norman, Benjamin had been able to successfully play an elusive game of catch-me-if-you-can. Unfortunately, his luck finally ran out. Norman was a cold-blooded predator who could spot his prey from a distance. He had many, but today Benjamin was the chosen one. To Norman's luck and Benjamin's dismay, the halls were left unmonitored as students filed out of their classes for lunch break. Spotting the flaw in the school's security system, Norman was standing in wait as Benjamin turned the corner at the audio-visual room. Without saying a word, he grabbed Benjamin in a headlock and began to consistently feed him punches until he fell like a sack of potatoes to the floor. As Norman's knuckles connected with Benjamin's stomach, he did not try to defend himself; he was no match for Norman's mammoth size nor his trained wrestling skills. To add insult to injury, Norman reached down and removed his left hearing aid from his ear. Norman used his heavy foot to stomp on Benjamin's device and then he kicked it in the direction of the garbage bins. Norman was never satisfied with just beating his victims, he always had to leave a lasting impression of his damage. It had all happened so fast, the corridors were bustling, but Norman had avenged Benjamin's disrespect to him.

"Do not play with me dumb boy!" he shouted as he bolted off with a group of his followers loyally trailing him.

Writhing on the floor, Benjamin recognized the voice of Mr. Phillips asking, "Are you ok Benjamin?"

Being the only deaf student in the school, the principal was familiar with Benjamin. The shouts of "fight, fight, fight" from the enthusiastic bystanders had alerted him that something was wrong.

"Yes… yes… sir," Benjamin stuttered.

He was in a pile on the floor, but he said the only thing he could have said in that moment. Norman had already done his deed and had made a clean escape. Benjamin tried to get up, but slumped back down to the floor.

Mr. Phillips extended his hand and helped him to his feet. His legs felt wobbly as he tried to regain his balance. The top button of his shirt was ripped off and patterns of dirt now decorated his freshly ironed uniform. Benjamin could have easily passed for an unkempt homeless person who rummaged through garbage bins trying to find anything of use.

"What has happened here?"

Mr. Phillips was speaking slowly as if he was thinking about what to say next. His face was a picture of concern when he saw the state that Benjamin was in. Benjamin wanted to tell him that Norman had done this to him, but he knew better than telling the principal the truth.

"I slipped and fell and lost my hearing aid during the fall," Benjamin mumbled.

Judging by Mr. Phillips' eyes, Benjamin knew that the principal knew that he was lying. But he could not risk telling him the truth. There were a few students still hanging in the hallway and they would tell Norman that he was a snitch. That would have only made the situation worse.

"Are you sure about that Benny?" asked Mr. Phillips. His voice was even more serious than before.

Yes… yes… sir," Benjamin responded nervously.

Benjamin raised his head, looking in the direction of the ceiling, trying to hide the glossiness that were present in his eyes. Angella was standing there with a big empty smile across her face. The smile was making him angry. She had never spoken to him, except that time when they were in the same science group for the midterm project. He could not imagine how anyone could ever tolerate her. She was always acting like a puppy, needing instructions all the time.

"Where did your hearing aid fall?" Mr. Phillips asked.

"Somewhere over there," Benjamin said, pointing to the corner where the rubbish bins were. The pain in his stomach was becoming unbearable and he had to clench his teeth to not scream out in agony.

Pulling his glasses down to the tip of his nose, Mr. Phillips stated, "That hearing aid must have wings. I can't imagine you falling here and your hearing aid landing over there."

"I don't know sir," Benjamin whimpered, while trying not to blink because if he did, the tears would come streaming down.

Mr. Phillips walked towards where Benjamin had pointed and pulled away the bins, sticking out his body trying not to let the rim of the drums rub against his clothes. There were empty pastry bags, soda bottles, ripped book leaves and other bits and ends in piles behind where the bins were kept. He bent down and slowly picked up the garbage from the floor and shook each piece before throwing it into the bins. Angella joined him in the search and was trying to look as dutiful as possible; each time she would bend over and pick up a piece of garbage. Benjamin was unsure of what to do with himself, so he just stood there watching them with both hands inside his pockets. Mr. Phillips and Angella were using their bare hands to rummage through the garbage. Angella picked up a donut bag which still had a piece of donut inside. She shook the bag and out fell the hearing aid. She gave a shriek and held the device as if finding it was her greatest accomplishment ever. Mr. Phillips praised her for her alertness, took the hearing aid from her and handed it to Benjamin.

"You need to be more careful. These things cost an arm and a leg, and the school won't be responsible if you lose them," Mr. Phillips said as he placed the device into Benjamin's hand.

Benjamin nodded in agreement.

"By the way, if you should ever need anything, my office door is always open."

As Mr. Phillips turned to walk back to his office, Benjamin could only force a feeble "yes sir", trying his best to hide the fear that was in his voice. He felt as if his already fragile life was just ripped into shreds.

Immediately, there was a lump in his throat and his heart was palpitating at the speed of a million beats per minute. His hearing aid was a mangled mess. The earmold that was usually inserted inside his ear was still attached to the plastic casing which had the microphone, amplifier, receiver and battery compartment that he wore behind his ear. However, the whole thing looked as if it had gone through a tornado. Benjamin knew that getting a replacement was going to be very expensive and his parents were going to skin him if he did not come up with a good excuse.

"Oh no! Can my day get any worse?" Benjamin whispered to himself. Thoughts of him locked in his room forever crossed his mind.

"How am I going to get out of this?"

He placed the hearing aid in his shirt pocket while contemplating his next move. Having a broken hearing aid was one thing but he did not want his teachers or parents to know that Norman was bullying him. There were just some things adults did not understand. Not everything could be fixed with a detention or a warning note. Benjamin believed that some things needed brute force and a broken hearing aid was enough to let him know that he needed to use brute force against Norman. In his heart, he knew that this was going to be his fight, he would have to think of a way to beat Norman at his own game. One way or another.

He did not stand in the hallway looking like a picture of defeat for much longer. Before he was ambushed by Norman, he was on his way to the noticeboard to see if he had gotten the role of Davy Jones. He was still anxious to see what role he would be playing. However, that did not seem possible now as each hunched-down step he took was more painful than the previous. Norman had aimed solely for his stomach. As a fulltime bully, Norman knew that it was best if he punched Benjamin in places that would not leave any visible scars or bruises. He had gotten enough detentions and warning notes to know this.

As much as Benjamin wanted to satisfy his curiosity, the pain was too excruciating, and he could not make it to the noticeboard. He made baby steps to the nearby bathroom to get himself together and escape the judgmental eyes of the same students who had watched Norman beat him mercilessly without trying to help. His stomach felt as if someone was reaching in and ripping him apart with a piercing tool. Small beads of sweat had formed a pattern on his forehead, and his eyes had started to tingle.

He hobbled into a stall and closed the door behind him. He sat on the closed toilet seat and started to sob. He was not sure where the tears came from, but they came as soon as he closed the door. The tears felt hot and sticky as they rolled down his cheeks. He was in pain, but the tears were not only from the punches that Norman had so wickedly inflicted, but also from the embarrassment that he felt. While crying in the bathroom stall, he was mindful of the humiliation it would bring if other students knew that he had gone there to cry. Every time he heard the bang of the door, he would bury his head inside his hands to keep the sounds muffled. Word spread fast and he did not want Norman to have the satisfaction of believing that he had triumphed over him.

"Did you see his face as Norman punched him?"

Two boys had entered the bathroom and they were gleefully discussing his beating. Benjamin was embarrassed, he did not want to show his face again, but he knew he could not stay hidden in the bathroom stall forever. He had to make the difficult decision to return to class when the bell sounded. The pain was still present as he walked up the staircase littered with after-lunch food wrappings. There were some uncomfortable stares and a few snickers. He was trying to be discreet, behaving as if nothing had happened, faking as if it was just another day. He pretended that he had not noticed them. Benjamin knew that he was the laughingstock of the school but there was nothing he could do about it in the moment. He would have given anything to go back to how his life was a few days ago when no one barely paid any attention to him, and he had both hearing aids working. He was almost invisible, and he much preferred it that way. He was just the deaf boy who did not have any friends and did not speak clearly. Thanks to Norman, he had suddenly become famous, all for the wrong reasons. He knew he had to devise the perfect plan to deal with Norman. Benjamin was determined to have the last laugh.

His body was in class, but his mind was focused on his own problems. He could not focus on the lesson because he was trying to come up with an explanation for the broken hearing aid and unkempt uniform. His mother made a fuss about every little thing and the condition of his clothes was enough to send her into hysteria. Not to mention when he told her about the broken hearing aid. Her anger was going to go through the roof. He had no idea what he was going to do.

The rest of the school day was passing in a blur of him copying notes from the whiteboard and completing tasks in his workbooks. He was in a daze until Mrs. Vassell decided that she was going to be a thorn in his side.

"Benjamin do you know the answer?" Mrs. Vassell's voice shook him from his stupor.

"Uhhhh… is it photosynthesis?" The class erupted in laughter.

In the history of stupid answers, there had never been a more stupid answer. His face became flushed with embarrassment as Willie fell to the floor laughing.

"Benjamin, I don't think you heard the question."

"No Mrs. Vassell," he confessed.

"I asked what the most dangerous game was," Mrs. Vassell said, staring at him piercingly.

They had just completed the story *The Most Dangerous Game* in their literature books and Benjamin had liked the story. He knew the answer to the question, but he had already started down the wrong road. There was no way the answer could have been photosynthesis, but he felt like it was too late to correct his answer. He sat there, staring at the pages of the story, having no greater wish than for the floor to open up and take him in. His day could not have gotten any worse. But it did.

"Benjamin, what was the major conflict in the story?" Mrs. Vassell asked again.

He wished Mrs. Vassell would not have asked him any more questions. He had already made a fool of himself, but obviously she was not satisfied.

"The major conflict is Raintord vertut Tarot," he answered shyly.

"You mean Rainsford versus Zaroff," Mrs. Vassell stated in a voice loud enough that even people who were not in the class could hear her.

The class erupted in laughter. Benjamin knew it was coming. He knew the laughter and ridicule were bound to happen. That was the exact reason he did not like this class or Mrs. Vassell. She was always trying to humiliate him, and he hated her guts for it. Because of his deafness, he experienced speech delay. It was hard for him to pronounce some words, especially those that had soft consonants. Whenever he tried to say a word such as skin, it would sound as if he is saying tin. The class would erupt in laughter and he would just stand there feeling like a dummy. Mrs. Vassell knew this, all the teachers knew this, but she just did not care. She once told him that she was a teacher and not a speech therapist.

When the bell sounded, he could not have been happier. He could hardly wait for his unlucky day to come to an end. One of Norman's friends who permanently smelled like dumplings fried in stale cooking oil, snickered when Benjamin walked past him. Lanay was waiting for him at the staircase landing when he exited the classroom. He wanted to find out why she was not at Jordan's party, but she wanted to talk about other things.

"I heard what happened to you today." The anger was written all over her face.

"It was not that bad," Benjamin said.

He tried to downplay the weight of the situation but Lanay was not convinced.

"What do you mean it was not that bad? Norman is a bully, and he needs to be dealt with," she said.

"What did you expect me to do, Lanay?"

She rolled her eyes to the back of her head and started to beat on her chest with one hand as she spoke. "If I, Lanay Jones were there, it would have been a different ending. Mr. Norman would have met his match."

She was of a small stature but that mouth of hers was like Goliath. The words coming from Lanay's lips and her body size were at odds, which made her utterances laughable. Benjamin could not imagine her confronting someone in grade seven, moreover confronting Norman who towered over his grade ten classmates. It was an unpleasant conversation which he did not care to continue. He tried to change the subject.

"Why didn't you come to the party?" he asked.

"Cause daddy was punishing me for calling the neighbor a blasted idiot." Lanay said this casually as if it were a common occurrence for her to call someone an idiot.

They had a moment of silence and for a second, Benjamin thought that the conversation about Norman was over. But he did not stop thinking about how he could get back at him. He imagined himself going up to Norman and slapping him in his face until his fingers left imprints on Norman's cheeks. There was a loud thunder as they walked into the schoolyard, an early sign of the coming rain. A dog was howling in the distance and this made Benjamin even more nervous because he knew that dogs only howled when something bad was about to happen. Lanay was biting down on her lip and then she unexpectedly said, "Benny you need to fight Norman. I will help you."

She was determined to have this conversation, but Benjamin was determined not to. He did not respond, that was the wise thing to do. Responding would only incite an argument. Moreover, they were almost at the gate and he did not want his mother to know that he and Lanay were having a disagreement. He did not want to have to tell her about Norman. He was already in enough trouble for one day.

"I got the part! I am going to be Davy Jones!"

Benjamin was almost dancing when he got to the tree.

"Lucky you," Lanay responded with her voice bereft of any type of joy.

The excitement which Benjamin had was clearly not being shared by Lanay. She was sitting with her back hunched on the stump of the tree, biting down on her lip. Whenever she was angry or deep in thought, she would bite down on her lip. She had not yet started to eat, and it did not seem like she was interested in eating at all. Her lunch bag was carelessly laying in the loose, red dirt.

"Do you want to exchange?" Benjamin asked.

He was offering her his coco-bread and patties in exchange for whatever she had in her lunch bag.

She pushed away his hand and said, "I don't want any coco-bread and patty."

She slid over, moving her body roughly along the tree bark. He took a seat beside her. She was still biting down on her lip and drawing patterns of O with her left foot in the dirt. Benjamin knew why she was angry, but he did not expect her to be this upset about it. He had already told her that she would not have gotten the role of Mowgli, but she had insisted.

"Lanay I told you that you would not have gotten the role. Why are you so angry?"

He was trying to rationalize the situation, but he only made things worse.

"Benjamin Morgan do I look angry to you? Only animals get angry." She paused for a second and then said, "As a matter of fact, I am going to show Mr. Phillips who is angry."

With that she stormed off, leaving him with her dusty lunch bag to wonder what she was up to. Lanay was like a jumbled word puzzle and he was not in any mood to try and unscramble her. He allowed his mind to settle and watch the ants as they carried off the crisp, yellow crumbs from the patty that had fallen to the ground.

It was not long afterwards Lanay stormed back to the tree carrying a pen and a piece of paper. She was still biting down on her lip when she plopped down beside Benjamin and snapped, "I am going to show all of them that there is no difference between boys and girls."

It was as if she had been preparing for this moment all her life. Thoughts seemed to be pouring from her brain and she was collecting them on paper in a letter addressed to Mr. Phillips.

Dear Mr. Phillips,

I am Lanay Jones, you will remember me from the meeting with my father, Ambassador Jones. I am extremely disappointed in the school for not choosing me to play Mowgli. I know that I was not chosen because I am a girl. Girls are just as good as boys in everything. I would have been the perfect choice. I practiced every day to be Mowgli and I know that I was perfect in the audition. Since your teachers do not think I am good enough to play Mowgli, then I do not want to be a student of this stupid school anymore. I am asking that you expel me so that my father can find a better school to put me in.

Lanay Jones

Before Benjamin could process what was happening, she folded the paper and wrote, *To The Principal, Mr. Phillips*, in bold, sloppy handwriting. As she was walking away, he felt as if the weight of the world was bearing down on his shoulders. He had to stop her.

"Lanay please don't! Don't do it Lanay!" Benjamin begged as he ran behind her, hoping she would change her mind. "You will get in trouble with Mr. Phillips."

The dull-eyed goat that Mr. Lewis kept on the property bleated as if it had recognized them as they walked by the shrub on which it was tied. Lanay hissed in irritation at both Benjamin and the goat, and began to walk more purposefully. They entered the hallway leading to the office and she was being relentless about her mission.

"I have already made up my mind, so don't even bother," Lanay said, brushing his hand off her shoulder.

She was approaching the principal's office and she seemed to be as focused as ever. She was not blinking. She was not biting down on her lip. Her face held no emotion as she pushed open the sprawling brown office door. Benjamin did not enter the office with her, he stood at the door and peeked inside to see what she was doing. She approached the large desk that was always littered with file jackets, bulky folders, and about one million sheets of paper that were in no order. The secretary was working at the computer behind the desk and did not raise her head to acknowledge her. He did not know what Lanay said to the secretary, but she pointed without raising her head to a little black box with the word 'received' written on it. Benjamin could feel his knees buckle under the pressure of what Lanay was about to do. He was immediately in an intolerable state of discomfort as she walked over to the box and dropped the letter in.

That was where his association with her ended for the day. He wanted no parts of the trouble that she was about to be in. There were still a few minutes left before the bell, but he decided it would be best if he returned to his classroom. Lanay exited the office in glory, smiling as if all of the anger and disappointment had left her body.

"I have to go back to class now. I need to complete my homework," Benjamin said to her.

She gave him a long pensive look before she said, "Suit yourself Mr. Morgan."

They parted company, going in opposite directions. Lanay went back in the direction of the tree where she had left her lunch bag. Benjamin did not want to be seen with her; not after what she had done.

He took the long way back to his classroom, walking up the staircase, past the gym and the detention room. Norman was in the detention room, sitting at a desk looking like a lost, lonely sheep. There was just something in his eyes that made Benjamin pity him in that moment. However, his feeling of empathy for Norman did not last long as he remembered that Norman was a monster and deserved everything bad that was happening to him. Benjamin's stomach was still sore from the whipping Norman had doled out to him the day before, there was no way he could feel sorry for Norman. Because of Norman, he was going to be grounded for three weeks. His father had taken his PlayStation 4 console with the controller and said he would get them back when he learnt to be more responsible. Benjamin's less than truthful excuse of falling while trying to catch the ball during a cricket game was not good enough for his parents.

The bell rang shortly after Benjamin got to class and everyone slowly filed to their seats. Ms. Samuels walked in wearing a blue skirt with a red cardigan on her tall, slender frame. Around her neck was a silver necklace with a strange pendant of an eye in a hand. It looked as if it was something she had acquired on one of her travel expeditions. Ms. Samuels was an interesting woman in a weird kind of way. She had the goal of traveling to at least fifty countries before she got too old to move around, as she liked to say. So far, she said she had been to nineteen countries. Benjamin did not think Ms. Samuels had any friends or family to share her travel stories with, and that was why she would share her stories with her students. Benjamin was curious, but he knew that any question about the pendant would prompt the longest story about its origins, since she was always so eager to impress her students. To Benjamin's dismay, Anice was just as curious about the pendant and asked Ms. Samuels about it.

"Ms. Samuels, what kind of pendant is that?"

It was not that Benjamin was not interested in the pendant, but they were supposed to start a new algebra topic and Benjamin was excited. His father had taught him everything he needed to know about linear equations, factoring and polynomials. He was anxious to show off his knowledge. Plus, mathematics was his favourite subject since it did not require him to read anything aloud.

"It is a Hand of Fatima. I bought it when I visited Morocco last year," Ms. Samuels beamed. "It provides me with protection and good luck."

There were hushed whispers of "Morocco!" as Mrs. Samuels did her pinched little smile of satisfaction. She had a weird way of smiling approvingly by squeezing her lips together in a pout. She would start a story and just as it was beginning to get interesting, she would take a pause, and wait for the students to beg to hear more. Just like that time she told them about meeting a ninth-generation cousin that looked just like her from the Masai tribe in Kenya, she had the students almost on their knees begging to hear more. The students were always impressed by Ms. Samuels' travel stories. She said that it was her way of breaking the ice, although Benjamin did not understand what she meant by breaking the ice. Deaf people sometimes had a difficult time understanding euphemisms.

As she was gearing up to delve into details about her trip to Morocco, Benjamin raised his hand and asked, "Ms. Samuels, what is the topic for today?"

"Oh, we will be solving equations with fractions," she said.

Ms. Samuels went to the whiteboard and was in the process of writing when the principal's booming voice came over the intercom.

"Lanay Jones, come to the principal's office now!"

Benjamin knew it was trouble, and very deep trouble too. Only when students were in trouble, were their names announced over the intercom system. He was fearful for Lanay and wished she had not gone out of her way to seek this problem. He just could not understand her. It was not hard to tell that Lanay was different from the rest of the students in the school. They were island children with island values, but it was not the same for Lanay. She was always talking about things that the other children in the school knew very little about, or even cared about. She had lived in Europe and Benjamin would sometimes criticize her for behaving like the mouthy foreign children he would see on television. Island children knew better than to talk back to adults, but Lanay seemed to have forgotten that she was not in Europe anymore.

Benjamin's final class for the day was general science. On the way to the laboratory, he had to walk past the principal's office. The door was partly opened, and he peeked inside to see if he could get a glimpse of Lanay. The secretary was at her untidy desk working at the computer, but there was no sign of Lanay anywhere.

She must be in Mr. Phillips' room at the back of the office, he thought.

What had irritated Lanay about not getting the role was beyond his comprehension. He did not have much experience with girls outside of his family, but he knew that Lanay was definitely a handful. This was not her first brush with the principal. Last month she was given a warning note when she threw a tantrum over a picture in her English textbook. As far as Benjamin was concerned, it was just a lousy picture of a man and a woman. The man was dressed in a white coat with a pair of stethoscopes around his neck, and the woman was standing by a sink doing dishes. Lanay got upset, ripped the picture from the book and threw it in the garbage in front of the teacher. She was firmly warned by Mr. Phillips for that transgression.

At the end of the school day, the skies had turned from a bright, cloudless blue to a gloomy, still grey, to match Benjamin's mood. His mother was waiting with Thomas in the car when he got to the gate. She was parked under the willow tree, with her back to the school. She did not see him coming and he was happy. On his way to the car, he had passed Lanay with her father standing at the secretary's desk, as if they were waiting for an important piece of paper. He did not want to have to explain to his mother why Lanay was not with him; she liked Lanay and he did not want to compromise that.

"Good evening mommy," Benjamin said as he opened the car door and took a seat beside Thomas in the back.

"Hey Benny!" She turned around displaying a bright, burgundy colour on her lips. "Are you ready to go and see Mr. Farad?"

He gave a quick nod and buckled his seatbelt as his mother started the car. Benjamin had an appointment with the audiologist to repair his hearing aid. He was managing with only one, but he was going to need both for the rehearsals and the musical.

As the car was driving away, Lanay and her father emerged from the school walking through the light rain sprinkles that were coming down. She was biting down on her lip and casually pulling her school bag behind her. Benjamin waved at her, but she did not wave back. He was not sure if Lanay had not seen him or she was just ignoring him. Although he had seen her father many times before, this was Benjamin's first time seeing him outside the car. He was a burly man who it seemed had never taken ten minutes of exercise in his life. He walked with the unease of a penguin and Benjamin could tell that he was more upset about having to walk to the principal's office, than for the reason he was called to the office. The car bent the corner, and they were no longer in view.

CHAPTER

9

"Sorry Benny, we will have to find another role for you."

Benjamin's life was falling apart and there was nothing he could do about it. His appointment with the audiologist did not go as well as he had expected. The microphone was broken, and the hearing aid would have to be sent to Canada for repairs. Mr. Farad was the only audiologist on this side of the island who also repaired hearing aids. The level of damage to Benjamin's device was outside of his capabilities and it needed overseas expertise.

"Another third world problem," his mother said disappointedly.

She was using her fingers to tug at her freshly done microbraids that were causing her discomfort along her hair edges. She had lived in London for a few years while studying for her law degree and because of this, she had the unintentional tendency to compare everything on the island with what she had experienced in London.

Mr. Farad, who Benjamin thought had a befitting name due to his large forehead, said that it would take six weeks for it to be returned. Having to go six weeks without one of his hearing aids was going to feel like forever. Benjamin looked about the brightly painted orange room, trying to think of something that could have helped his case. He could think of nothing; he had to accept his fate. His mother sensed his disappointment and gave his hand a tight squeeze as they left Mr. Farad's third floor office. Benjamin was disheartened that they had waited in traffic and had driven for almost two hours to receive such horrible news.

"Would you like to have some hot wings?" his mother asked.

He was staring through the car window, watching people go about their daily business.

"No ma'am," he said in the most depressive tone he could pull from the back of his throat.

Hot wings were his favorite, but he had no appetite. His mother was trying, but there was nothing she could do or say to remove the spear that was wedged in his heart. Thomas, being unaware of what was happening, did not have a care in the world. He was smiling, showing his two upper milk teeth that had recently broken through the gums and clapping his hands until he fell asleep. His mother tried to make small talk to lighten the mood, but the weight of the world was bearing down on his shoulders. A group of scruffy looking boys, about Benjamin's age or younger, bombarded the car window at the stoplight. They had their hands outstretched with the look of poverty evident in their blackened palms and beneath their fingernails. His mother reached inside her purse and pulled out a crisp five-hundred-dollar note and handed it to the smallest boy in the group. He grabbed the money and took off running before she could tell him how to divide it among his friends. The other boys took off after him, revealing rips and holes in their clothes.

"Those boys would do anything to get even half of what you have."

This was a conversation opener for his mother who was about to use the boys' misfortunes as an opportunity to remind Benjamin of how blessed he was. He slouched in the backseat, merely grunting and nodding as she spoke. She soon recognized his disinterest in whatever she was saying and gave up. The rest of the drive home was done in absolute silence. The musical would be coming up in four weeks, rehearsals were scheduled to begin soon, and he did not know what to do.

The following morning, Benjamin tried to reason with Mrs. Kennedy, but she was not convinced that he could play the part of Davy Jones without both working devices. He stood at her table, begging her to let him keep his role, but she ignored him, turning the pages of her romance novel as he spoke. He stared at her, wondering what major difference having one hearing aid, or two hearing aids really made. He knew that wearing two hearing aids would increase the range and distance of his hearing, but he was sure he could manage with only one. He strolled from the drama room, closing the door heavily behind him as he left. Once again, it was proven that his mother's belief that he was the captain of his own ship was wrong. He was trying to steer his own ship, but it had run aground. Mrs. Kennedy's decision was final.

Benjamin was disappointed, there was no other role for him, plus it was not fair. He had auditioned for the role of Davy Jones and had gotten it, fair and square. He thought he was the unluckiest person in the world. He was so disappointed that he started to think about Ms. Samuels' Hand of Fatima. He wondered if it had the same good luck as the magical charms he had seen in movies. Not that he had any chance of finding out. He could not go to Ms. Samuels and say, "Can I get some of the magic from your pendant?" Besides, he believed that magic was as real as mermaids.

"Pssshhh," he hissed as he walked to his class.

His detour to Mrs. Kennedy's drama room had made him late for science class. The morning air was hot and still although the sun had not too long ago made its eastern debut. He felt no need to hurry and his walking said so. Summer was quickly approaching, and it seemed as if his body was losing tons of water by the minute in the morning heat. Lines of sweat trailed down his back and settled at the pants waist, held by his belt. As late as he was, he had to make a choice between dying from dehydration or rehydrate and be punished by Mr. Williams for his tardiness to class. He stopped to get some water.

"Boy, hurry and fill that bottle, and get to class!"

It was Mr. Phillips' voice urging Benjamin to move along. He was bent over at the fountain, swallowing big gulps of cold water directly from the cooler. It was the school's policy to only use recyclable water bottles, but he no longer carried one. He hated the idea of walking around with a water bottle; there was just something about it that was too effeminate and girlish for him. He had sprouted three strands of hair on his chin and was determined to protect the sanctity of the man he was becoming.

He had his fill of water and hurried off to class before Mr. Phillips returned.

"What do honey, toothpaste, paint and ketchup have in common?"

That was the question being asked by Mr. Williams when Benjamin got to class. He was expecting to receive a detention for being tardy, but Mr. Williams only nodded and continued speaking when he entered and took his seat. The question seemed to be some sort of riddle and Benjamin did not have the slightest clue of what the answer could have been.

Willie stuck up his hand and said, "They all have different colors."

He was expecting howls of laughter, but the students knew better. They did not want to have to spend their entire lunch break in detention. Mr. Williams ignored Willie and asked the question again.

This time Florence stuck her hand up. "They behave at times like a solid and at times like a liquid."

Florence was a shy, soft-spoken girl who was always reading. Through a divine stroke of luck, she was nominated to be the president of The Debate Club. Benjamin still could not understand how she functioned as president when she hardly spoke.

"You are right, Florence," Mr. Williams said. "These substances do not follow Newton's law of viscosity."

Benjamin had heard about Newton before, but this was his first-time hearing about viscosity. However, he need not worry even with one hearing aid. There had never been a more committed science teacher than Mr. Williams. Benjamin imagined that when he was younger, Mr. Williams was like the cartoon character Dexter, who was always whipping up world-saving inventions in his secret laboratory. Dexter had grown up to be Mr. Williams and his students were his proteges who he frequently had looking through microscopes or combining substances to bring the classes alive.

"Today, you will be working in pairs to conduct an experiment on viscosity," Mr. Williams said.

There were hushed whispers as the students scurried to find the perfect partner for the experiment. Melody and Reina were arguing about who first said they would be working with Florence. Florence decided that she would not be working with neither of them and pulled her desk to join Brittany's. Akeem was sitting next to Benjamin and they had an unsaid agreement that they would be working together.

Mr. Williams was weaving in and out between desks and chairs. With each group, he left a jar containing either honey, toothpaste, ketchup, oil, or water. He explained that viscosity can either be high or low, as he handed each group a marble. On the count of three they were to drop the marbles into the jars to measure the speed in which the marbles sank to the bottom of the jars. The class was quietly engaged in the experiment when there was a loud crash. There was a scuffle between Willie and Leon; they were on the ground clawing at each other like wild animals.

"Boys you need to stop at this minute!" Mr. Williams shouted as he approached the chaos.

He was trying his best to separate them, but his short stature could not pull the towering teenaged boys apart. Danny and Errol who were sitting at the back, had to intervene to take Leon off Willie. Their uniforms were disheveled and were a mixture of dirt and oil when they were dragged to their feet.

"Both of you look like something the cat dragged in!" Mr. Williams said furiously.

"It is Willie's fault, sir. He started it." Leon was drenched in oil and was grasping for breath as he sought to explain his side of the story.

"Enough! We are going to the principal's office right now," Mr. Williams said.

Bright red blood oozed from the right corner of Willie's mouth. He did not try to say anything. His right eye was swollen and seemed to be doing an involuntary dance. Mr. Williams led them out of the classroom, leaving the rest of the students on their own to wonder which substances had high viscosity and which had low viscosity.

During the squabble between Leon and Willie, Benjamin saw Norman and his classmates walking down the staircase with their library cards. The class lesson on viscosity had come to a premature end which gave Benjamin the opportunity to go on his own little mission. He quickly removed the gift box secured in a black plastic bag from his knapsack, and made a quick run to Norman's grade ten classroom. It was not hard for him to find Norman's desk. Mr. Thorne was Norman's homeroom teacher, and he was known to walk around the school with his labelling machine affixing names and dates to things that did not even concern him. He behaved as if the labelling machine was some sort of mysterious device which could solve all of the world's problems. Norman's desk was at the back of the room and looked like a disaster area. Huge drawings and unrecognizable writings covered every inch of the small table. Thanks to the weekly birthday section on the noticeboard, Benjamin had become aware of Norman's birthday being only a few days away. Benjamin was leaving the perfect gift for him.

The grass was still damp when Benjamin got to the playfield. Lanay was already at the tree and was sitting down on a piece of paper covering the wet tree root. The leaves danced above their heads in the light wind left by the all-night rain. He was anxious to hear what happened yesterday in the meeting with Mr. Phillips and her father. He also needed to tell her that he was no longer going to be Davy Jones because of his broken hearing aid. She was more anxious to talk than he was, she did not even give him a chance to sit before she started.

"Mr. Phillips said that I have to write an apology letter for assembly on Friday morning."

"What did your father say?" Benjamin asked.

"He said I'd have to do it on my own," Lanay replied.

Coincidentally they both had brought bun and cheese for lunch. A group of grade seven girls had inched closely to the tree to start a lively game of skipping. The rope made a distinctive plop, plop, plop sound each time it landed on the muddy ground.

"You will have to help me to write the apology," she told Benjamin.

Lanay had this unbothered way of telling people that they had to do what she wanted. Her orders were not given in aggression, but she said them in a way that gave you no choice. She removed a crumpled sheet of paper and a pen from the lunch bag she was holding in her lap.

"What am I going to write Bennnyyy?" she said, dragging out the last letters of his name as she unfolded the paper.

"Ummm… just say that you are sorry," he said, biting into the sweet bun.

"It can't just be I am sorry; it has to be perfect," Lanay said.

She looked out in the distance and slightly tilted her head to the right before biting down on her lip. The girls were still there playing. The tall girl was now in the middle jumping as two other girls methodologically spun the rope. Her knees seemed to go to the height of her shoulders as the rope passed under her muddy shoes. Small balls of red mud flew in the air behind her, others attaching themselves to her blue tunic.

"I know what I will write!" Lanay exclaimed.

She was smiling as if something good was about to happen.

The smile made Benjamin uncomfortable as she put the pen to paper. Friday was only a day away, there was no time to waste.

Dear Mr. Phillips,

I am writing to you today to apologize for hurting your feelings, and not because I think I did something wrong.

Benjamin glanced over at the paper and had the same sick feeling that he had had when she dropped the first letter in the little black box.

"Lanay you can't write that," he said.

He was attempting to take the paper from her hand, but she quickly hid it behind her back. A strong wind came by which sent big blobs of water that had accumulated on the leaves onto their heads. She waited for a few seconds before she placed the now damp paper on her lunch bag and continued to write.

I understand that in life people can make very poor choices and leave others to make up for their mistakes. I still do not want to be Mowgli because I am too smart to be acting like a jungle boy anyway. I am getting ready to go back to Belgium to live with my mother and sister. I hate…

He felt a soft panic as the words flowed onto the paper. Lanay's face was rigid with tension and gave a hint of pent up emotions. It seemed as if she was upset about something more than not being chosen to be Mowgli. Whatever it was, he was her friend and he felt he had a duty to stop her from getting herself into more trouble. He placed the half-eaten bun and cheese into his brown paper bag, and took a drink of the lukewarm soda which he had in his lap, before placing it inside the paper bag. Without a word, he grabbed the paper from Lanay's unexpecting hands, summoned the speed of a cheetah and took off running. Short grasses glistened with water along the sides of the foot-beaten path as he sped away. The thick red mud felt slushy and slippery underneath his sneakers. He had dared not look back to see if Lanay was chasing after him until he got to the corridor. Benjamin turned around with the torn paper in his hand, but she was nowhere in sight. He rolled up the paper, placed it in his pocket and climbed the stairs to his second-floor classroom. He would have to avoid the staircase landing and use the backdoor emergency exit after school.

CHAPTER 10

The wind from the industrial fans whipped her ponytail as she took a deep, long breath. She was walking slowly as if each step required great thought and effort. She looked even smaller for her age reaching for the microphone on the lectern, by standing on her tiptoes. Benjamin had said a silent prayer when her name was called to come to the stage, but he was of little faith. Lanay was unpredictable and it only required the right amount of accumulated anger for her to go off. Silence overcame the auditorium as she twisted her face like she was in great pain. She gazed intensely at the crowd before placing the microphone to her unsmiling mouth.

"Good morning everyone." Her voice was trembling. She took a pause and swallowed loudly in the microphone before continuing.

"I am Lanay Jones. I want to apologize to Mr. Phillips for the letter I wrote to him. What I did is inexcusable, and I deeply regret my action. In the future I will practice more restraint."

The apology was said in one prolonged breath. There was no fluff or indirect jabs at Mr. Phillips like she had attempted to do yesterday. It was short and to the point. Benjamin knew her well enough to know that it was not written by her, but he was relieved. The pseudo apology was good enough for him. He hoped that would be the end of her quest to be Mowgli or to shame the school for their decision to not choose her.

Her eyes were fixed on the brown parquet floor of the stage as she placed the microphone on the lectern. Mr. Phillips lightly patted her left shoulder as if to say all was forgiven. The auditorium were a mixture of chuckles and sparing applauses as she walked off the stage in fast stomping steps. Silent tears were rolling down her cheeks when she walked past Benjamin's class line to join hers. He kept his eyes fixed on her. He could not believe cantankerous Lanay was crying because she had to read a few words from a paper. As the final announcements were being read, he quietly moved over to where she was standing in line with the grade seven students. He felt helpless and was unsure of what to do next. The whirring sound of the oscillating blades from the fans seemed to had gotten louder as he stood there in silence. Lanay was still sobbing and it made Benjamin uncomfortable. He attempted to squeeze her hand as they walked out of the auditorium to go to their classes.

"Leave me alone Benny," she said before pulling away.

She flounced up the stairs to her classroom at an angry pace. Her face was blotchy and puffy, with faint teeth marks on her bottom lip. Benjamin had never seen Lanay look so defeated and it deeply affected him. He could not stop thinking about her throughout his morning class sessions. He made up an excuse about having to use the bathroom, just so he could walk past her classroom to see how she was doing. The door was closed and not a sound was coming from inside. He returned to his class disappointed. Not even Ms. Samuels' ice-breaking story about swimming with dolphins in the clear, blue waters of Sharm El Sheikh could change his mood.

He ran to the tree at recess. Lanay was already there and she was in a much better spirit. Her face was no longer blotchy and puffy, but had returned to a healthy olive tone. She was sitting under the tree eating a pack of ginger cookies. A bee was buzzing around the syrupy liquid she had in the opened bottle next to her.

"Daddy forced me to read the stupid apology he wrote last night," she said without being asked.

"It was not stupid. It was okay," Benjamin replied, hoping to defuse any residual anger or tears.

She did not say anything and continued to eat her cookies. The wind rustled the leaves above their heads, announcing the coming rain. He sat down beside her and noticed that on her feet she was wearing a pair of pink rubber boots that she was not wearing at devotion, nor did it go well with the blue and white uniform. In the school's code of conduct booklet, it had boldly stated that students were only allowed the school colors of blue, black and white. It was nearing the hurricane season and there had been frequent rainfall, but despite this, Benjamin knew that she was using the current weather condition to get back at the school. He did not comment on her pink boots, but it was like an elephant in the room and she sought to give an explanation.

"I think it is going to rain, so I changed my shoes. I do not want to ruin my leather loafers," she said.

Benjamin took his sandwiches from his brown paper bag and started to eat. He gave Lanay the pack of Skittles he had brought for her as a reconciliation gift for what he had done yesterday. She opened the packet and threw a rainbow of flavors into her hand. The gale winds were getting stronger and was causing green leaves to fall from the branches, some still attached to their twigs. She threw the handful of the sour-sweet candy into her mouth, then licked her palm, smeared with colours. She was chewing slowly and was using her tongue to pry off the candy that had attached themselves to her incisors. She reached for the bottle of syrupy drink only to realize that the bee had ventured inside and was floating atop the cold liquid.

"Stupid bee! I did not want it anyway," she said, before emptying the contents onto the ground.

She walked past the same group of girls still playing skipping and threw the empty bottle into the bin for recycled plastic. She took her water bottle from her bag and had a drink of the icy liquid.

Benjamin was also thirsty after eating three corned beef sandwiches and reached for his water bottle from his paper bag. Lanay gave him a startled look as if she had just seen a ghost and then she started to giggle.

"I thought you no longer used a bottle because it is too effeminate," she said between giggles.

"It is more convenient to have it, than not to have it," Benjamin said in his defense.

He was trying to save face and wished he had never made that proclamation to Lanay because she could not stop laughing. Mr. Lewis was walking past the tree with a bunch of bananas balanced on a rounded piece of cloth on his head. He did not stop but waved to them and laughed with Lanay as if he understood her joke.

"I won't be Davy Jones anymore," Benjamin said, trying to make Lanay stop laughing.

Lanay stopped laughing and with the seriousness of a high court judge she said, "You are lying."

"I am being serious, Lanay," he responded. "Mrs. Kennedy says that I will need both hearing aids to play the part."

She popped her eyes wide open and brought her chin down to her chest in an expression of stunned surprise. "But you are functioning well with only one," she said, mentioning his hearing aids for the first time.

"That is because I was lucky. I have a higher hearing threshold in the left ear, more sound waves are captured in this ear. If it were the right hearing aid, I would not be able to function so well."

There was a loud, crashing thunder which sent the skipping girls scampering off into various directions. Their feet slapped the moist ground, leaving imprints of their shoe soles. Lanay did not react to the thunder, not that Benjamin was expecting her to. She often expressed revulsion for girls who were too tender, always behaving as if they needed to be saved from something. She did not say anything but took up the remaining Skittles and shook them in the bag while humming the tune to Jingle Bells, although Christmas was months away.

After a few seconds of humming, she asked, "So, what are you going to do Benny?"

He was not sure as yet, but his mother had suggested he ask to be the sign language interpreter at the show. She thought it would be a good way to show off his abilities and maybe some students would become interested in learning how to sign. When he explained this to Lanay, to his surprise she thought it would be a great idea.

"You could even start the school's first sign language club," she suggested. "And I could be your assistant."

Her eyes sparkled as she spoke. She had allowed her imagination to run away and was insisting that he teach her the basics of hand speaking.

"How do I say idiot?" She had gotten up and was standing in front of Benjamin with her hands wide open as if she were consulting a palm reader.

"Idiot is not basic, Lanay," Benjamin said.

She was getting ready to argue but he reminded her that he was the teacher. After a short discussion, they agreed that the alphabet would be a good place to start.

"First you have to fold your fist, then stick out your thumb like you are giving a thumb's up," he instructed. "By the way, the palm is always held forward."

"Like this Benny?" she asked.

"No, that is S not A."

She had incorrectly lapped her thumb over the bent fingers of her right hand. After ten minutes, the lesson with his new student – and soon to be assistant – was progressing at the speed of a snail's race. She kept on confusing the signs for b and d, rendering it impossible for them to get past the fourth letter of the alphabet.

"Tomorrow we will continue," he said after what seemed like an eternity of going over the same four letters.

She did not agree with his suggestion, but he was growing impatient with her. Another bee was circling the half-eaten skittles she had left carelessly laying open on the tree root. She took up a fallen branch and swatted at the pesky insect but missed. She took another handful of Skittles before continuing with her plans. The sign language club had suddenly become the focal point of her life and her intentions for it were endless.

"We should have the club on Tuesdays during lunch-break… We can seek permission to use the audio-visual room… and we should start making posters inviting members."

There was a long gurgling thunder which forced her to stop speaking. The sky had turned to a dark grey, draining away the light of the afternoon. The skipping girls had not returned to their game, and more students had packed up their belongings and were hurrying back to the main building. The playground supervisors were still in their positions, strutting around with their hands held behind their backs, looking out for trouble that was not there. Lanay had more plans for the club and resumed her proposals after the thunder.

"We should make a list of rules for the club… maybe we could even have a fundraiser for deaf children in need of hearing aids."

Drops of rain came cascading from the clouds, forcing them to immediately grab their lunch bags and run. The large drops stung their skin and quickly soaked through their uniforms. Mr. Lewis' goat was bleating as if it were experiencing its last moments on the butcher's table. The panic from the huge drops and the sudden bursts of thunder, had caused him to get into a fit, wrapping his rope too many times around the shrub he was tied to. They got to the bustling corridor and took a minute to catch their breath, sheltered from the rain. A funny-looking boy, older than Benjamin, missed his step and fell facedown in the clumpy mud. He was struggling to get to his feet, but the heavy mud and the pouring rainfall kept him captive on the ground. Another boy ran to his assistance, pulling him up but making a great deal of fuss over his lack of precision. The fallen boy looked like a pig who had just taken a partial mud bath. There were scattered chuckles as he joined the group on the corridor with a piece of mud hanging from his eyelid. The bell sounded and Lanay and Benjamin took the northern staircase back to their classrooms. The hall monitors were handing out squares of paper towel which were used to soak up some of the water from their bodies. There was no more time for Lanay to continue with her plans for the club, and Benjamin was happy. The paper towels did not help much but they had to go back to their classes. Benjamin thought Lanay was done talking but as she walked away, she turned around and said the last thing he was thinking about.

"Nauseating Norman does not bother you anymore, but you still have to fight him."

CHAPTER

11

Dear Parents of The Pirates of the Caribbean Musical,
We are delighted to announce that your child has been successful in his/her recent audition, and has been offered a part as a member of the cast or crew in the forthcoming production of Pirates of the Caribbean. He/she has been sent a separate letter with details of the assigned role.

Main rehearsals will take place during performing arts lessons, and some lunch breaks. Main characters must also be available to rehearse on Wednesday afternoons from 12.45 – 14.45, although they may not all be required each week. Details will be posted weekly on the school's website.

Yours sincerely,
Kelly Kennedy
Performing Arts Teacher

Benjamin's role as Davy Jones had gone to Patrick, but he had been given an even better role. His mother had written a letter to Mrs. Kennedy, and she had agreed that he be the speech language interpreter. As far as Benjamin was concerned, that was going to be the most important role at the musical. He was going to be the only person who was always going to be onstage. He had to know the scripts of everyone who was going to be performing and be ready to awe the crowd with his uncommon ability. In a way, he felt as if he was going to be having his Paul Dore moment.

His luck was finally changing, and he was sitting on top of the world. To make things even better, for the past few days Norman was being avoided like the plague. People would pinch their nostrils together, clench their faces and make a hasty retreat as soon as he was approaching. Norman's bullying behavior was not the cause of this reaction, in fact his assaults had decreased. The stench he carried was enough to make even a crocodile vomit. He smelled like dirty socks, rotten eggs, weeks old cabbage water and fish guts all mixed together. His huge following had been reduced to only Buster, who seemed to always be in a state of perpetual confusion. No matter how bad things got with Norman, Buster would still be running behind him like his lapdog. The tides had begun to change for Norman, he was becoming better known for his stench than his victims. He reeked so badly that he eventually got the nickname Nauseating Norman.

Norman's reaction to his nickname was not what Benjamin had expected. He had suddenly become a simple boy with civilities. His loud aggression was replaced by an almost shy fragility. That was what he demonstrated that morning when Benjamin encountered him in the nurse's quarters. Benjamin had gone to the nurse for her to administer a drop of medicine for another one of his annoying swimmer's ear infections. He was sitting alone on the long wooden bench in the small white room and was waiting for his name to be called. He had his eyes following a fly that had come in through the open door. The fly was dipping and diving as if it were doing a spiritual dance at a Pocomania church. Nurse Langley was taking forever to call him into the examination room, and he was overcome with boredom. Benjamin started studying the posters of different body parts and health recommendations that were glued to the wall. Even the fly eventually got bored with its monotonous dance, and rested on the poster bearing the picture of a smiling girl washing her hands at a sink.

Norman walked in, holding himself like he was trying to take up less space. His scent preceded him, and Benjamin had to hold his breath to prevent himself from passing out. Norman accidentally bumped his foot on Benjamin's outstretched leg which caused him to trip and land facedown on the shiny tiles. In the commotion, Norman had brought down the stack of magazines that were laying on the coffee table. His expression was of shock and horror as he struggled to his feet.

"I am sorry," Norman said as he hastily gathered the books scattered on the floor.

Benjamin was taken aback by his reaction. He wondered if Norman had realized that it was him, 'Benny the dummy' whose leg had sent him crashing to the floor. Norman's eyes were fixed to the tiles like he was too afraid or embarrassed to look up. He was sweating and his scent was rising. The fly left its position on the poster and settled on his head. Benjamin found this funny and chuckled. Even when Benjamin chuckled, Norman's eyes were still focused on the ground like he did not have a bullying bone in his body.

Nurse Langley walked out of her examination room spraying fumes of air freshener into the waiting area. She scrunched up her nose and made a comment about a rat dying in the room before looking at the file she was holding in her hand. Nurse Langley was a medium sized, racially ambiguous woman who it seemed was mixed with everything. She had curly blonde hair, slanted beady eyes, a long-humped nose, and thick lips.

"Benjamin Morgan, come this way," she said, pointing at the green door leading to the examination room.

She removed the vial with the antibiotic from the refrigerator and made a few jottings in the file she had rested on the table.

"Now hold still Benjamin," Nurse Langley said.

She made two drops in his left ear, taking great care not to contaminate the dropper. The liquid felt cold as it entered his ear canal, causing his throat to itch. Benjamin had to wait for a few minutes with his head tilted to the left before Nurse Langley could administer the drop into his other ear. The wind was blowing, and it carried Norman's odor into the examination room. Nurse Langley got up from her chair and got busy pulling out desk drawers and file cabinets while complaining again about a dead rat. She found nothing and stopped searching. The final drops of medication were administered to the left ear by a still bothered Nurse Langley. Benjamin waited with his head tilted in the other direction for two minutes, after which Nurse Langley cleaned his single hearing aid and reminded him to keep his ears away from dirt and moisture. On the way out, Benjamin passed Nauseating Norman still sitting on the wooden bench, removing a bottle of spray from his shirt pocket. He applied a few spray mists over his body, capturing the essence of the mixture in the fancy red bottle.

The ear infection was minor, but it prevented Benjamin from going to the tree. He had to keep away from dust, pollen, moisture, or anything that could further irritate his ears. This was his second infection since he had started swimming lessons four months ago. Lanay was not enthused about spending her lunch break in the canteen but she understood and agreed to go with Benjamin. There was usually a jostle to find an empty place to sit at one of the tables, which was partly the reason they chose to spend their lunchtimes at the mango tree. As their luck would have it, there was an unoccupied table with three chairs in the center of the room. Lanay hurried over and placed her lunch bag on the blue iron top table, marking it as their territory. Benjamin had stopped by the watercooler at the front of the room to refill their bottles and take in the chaos of the room. The canteen lady Ms. Rose, who was not a rose by any means, was sitting at her usual spot at the door and barking orders at everyone. The new worker, a yellow-skin girl of no more than twenty years was behind the counter looking like a deer caught between headlights. The sound of Ms. Rose's voice frightened her, causing her eyes to pop and slight tremors take over her body. She was constantly wiping her sweaty palms on the pockets of her soiled off-white apron, preventing the line from moving as quickly as it should.

For some reason, this irritated Ms. Rose more than it should have and her deep masculine voice permeated every inch of the buzzing room. Her excessive shouting had caused the new girl to become so nervous, she dropped the ladle she was using to scoop out big spoonfuls of chicken-foot soup with cornmeal dumplings and ground provisions into the bowls of waiting students who had paid for school lunches. The spoon landed with a big bang and sent splashes of the yellow liquid all over the floor and onto the girl's already soiled apron.

"You foolish girl!" shouted Ms. Rose at the girl who had gone from a high yellow colour to a bright pink. "You better clean this mess up right now!"

The girl stood frozen, unsure of what to do. Ms. Rose had a mouth which was already too big for her face but when she was angry, her mouth seemed to take over the full breadth of her face. Another canteen worker who they called Fin-Hand due to one arm being substantially shorter than the other, was alerted of the commotion and ran from the back kitchen carrying a bucket and mop. He tried to hand the cleaning tools to the new girl but on realizing she was in a state of shock and was in no haste to return to reality, he set the bucket down and started to wipe the soup off the floor in hurried circular motions. Behind the counter had deteriorated into pure disorder.

The line of hungry students was growing, which caused the ire of Ms. Rose. She was shouting even louder but did not move from her seated position on the tall stool at the door overlooking the happenings in the room. The girl was still standing in a stupor and Ms. Rose was noisily condemning her for her carelessness in the room full of curious students. Fin-Hand, who was Ms. Rose's longest serving staff, was trying to neutralize the situation by tapping the shoulder of the now crying girl. Unexpectedly, she snatched off the apron and cap revealing her perfectly cornrowed hair, and placed them on the counter in a heap. She ran to the back of the kitchen and moments later, she busted through the door which separated students from canteen workers revealing unpacked boxes of water, sodas, and other bits and ends on the floor. Her mid-length pleated dress bounced about her chubby legs as she ran through the swinging lunchroom doors and down the hallway as if her life depended on it. The muscles in Ms. Rose's face became tense as she was once again in the predicament that she frequently found herself. She would have to find another worker.

Benjamin joined Lanay at the table to have the rice and chicken his mother had packed for him. The waiting students were not being served and they had begun to get impatient. Ms. Rose, realizing the weight of her problem, instructed a sweating Fin-Hand to set down the mop, fetch a clean ladle and resume serving. He set off in a walk-run and in a few seconds a grinning Fin-Hand returned from the back with ladle in hand to embark on his new position as server in the canteen. It seemed as if it was not Fin-Hand's destiny to get this promotion. It was either excitement or forgetfulness that caused him to step onto the wet floor mindlessly, causing him to lose his balance and send him sprawling with his hands and feet in the air. One girl was brave enough to let a loud laughter escape her lips. Ms. Rose gave her a poisonous stare before shouting "Get out!", pointing to the swinging doors. The girl left her partially eaten soup, picked up her orange juice and walked out of the lunchroom without protesting. There was a tense silence as they watched the girl's back leave the room.

"Today must be the day for falling," Benjamin whispered.

"What do you mean?" Lanay asked.

He pretended not to hear her question because he did not want to have to go into details about Norman. In fact, he did not even want their names to be mentioned in the same sentence at this time. It was not hard to ignore Lanay without her asking again. The whole lunchroom was focused on the spectacle that was taking place behind the counter. Fin-Hand's bad luck provoked the wrath of Ms. Rose who instead of helping him to his feet, grabbed the ladle from his outstretched hand. She stepped over his body and proceeded to pour the soup into the bowls in big sloppy spoonfuls.

It was not hard to see why the lunchroom was constantly in need of workers. Ms. Rose was an intimidating woman. Her Amazonian height alone was enough to give anyone the creeps, but what made it worse was that her temper was hotter than a Middle Eastern summer. Plus, she walked with a slight hunch and never seemed to have anything in her life so pleasant, it would cause her to smile. She was always in a bad mood and had this way of staring as if her eyes were magnifying glasses, examining every inch of your presence.

Fin-Hand had managed to get back to his feet and ashamedly hobbled back to his rightful place in the back kitchen, holding his backside. Ms. Rose portioned out the lunches to the waiting students who dared not complain about how many dumplings or pieces of meat they were getting, as they had done with the new girl. It was obvious that she was in a sour mood, and no one wanted to be the recipient of her wrath. They all sat in silence and ate their lunches, afraid to even breathe loudly, moreover speak. Lanay did not make any mention of the sign language club, so she and Benjamin sat in silence, making oaths to themselves that not even an ear infection could cause either of them to eat under the watchful eyes of Ms. Rose ever again. An embattled Fin-Hand emerged from the back to clear the tables of empty cups and bowls. The back of his pants were wet as if he had given the bruised area a run under cold water. The bell rang and the students filed out of the canteen orderly and tense, leaving an upset Ms. Rose sitting on her stool complaining about the impossibility of finding good help these days.

CHAPTER

12

ncle George was the last person Benjamin was expecting to see when he got home from school on Wednesday afternoon. His mother had been very smiley and secretive when she came to meet him at the school gate, but he was not expecting this surprise. Uncle George looked smart in the forest-green button-down shirt, green pants, and green loafers. He looked like a government official sitting in Benjamin's father's rocking chair with one leg crossed at the knee over the other. He smiled brightly when Benjamin walked in. His symmetrical face seemed to have filled out which made him look more manly and strong. So much seemed to have changed about Uncle George since the last time Benjamin had seen him. It was still Uncle George, tall and lean, but there was just something that made him different.

"How's it Benny?" he asked.

"Better than I had expected," Benjamin replied.

Uncle George threw his head back and started to laugh hysterically. His laugh was contagious which made Benjamin laugh too. His mother knitted her brows, looking confused from Uncle George to Benjamin. There was nothing said in her presence which had warranted such hysterical laughter, but neither of them was going to make her any the wiser. She sucked her teeth the way Caribbean women normally did to show their displeasure before walking from the room.

This was Benjamin's second time seeing Uncle George since receiving the whipping from Norman. On the afternoon of his defeat, when he got home, he used his mobile phone to call Uncle George and tell him about the colossal embarrassment Norman had caused him. Benjamin was so angry, he told his uncle that he wished Norman had lost more than just his sense of smell in the wrestling incident. That was when Uncle George got the idea of utilizing his knowledge of fragrances to give Norman a whiff of his own medicine. Two days later, Uncle George visited and secretly gave Benjamin a package wrapped in silver paper to be specially delivered to Norman. Benjamin had an idea but was not sure exactly what Uncle George had placed inside the package. He told Benjamin it was some sort of perfume that he had made, along with a wristband and a pair of socks. Benjamin was excited; Uncle George's idea for getting back at Norman was better than anything he could have planned or fighting Norman as Lanay had suggested.

Uncle George's current surprise visit was not without cause. He had come to bid farewell to Benjamin, Thomas and their parents. He broke the news to the family that he had applied online for an engineering job with a car company in Munich, Germany and was successful. This revelation was a shocker to Benjamin. He never imagined Uncle George ever agreeing to live anywhere except for his grandparents' home. The thought of his uncle deciding to go and live thousands of miles away was distressing to him. The heat in the house had suddenly become overwhelming for Benjamin. The muscles in his face started to quiver, and he was struggling to breathe. He walked over to the open window, hoping the breeze coming in through the fluttering chiffon curtains could somehow soothe him.

"Are you alright Benny?" his uncle asked.

He was attempting to hide his grief, but the feeling of loss left a hole in his stomach. Uncle George sensed what was happening and gently placed his hand on Benjamin's shoulder. The sadness came rolling in like waves lashing the corner of his eyes. If he had attempted to respond, his voice would have been a quavering muddle of talking and crying. Without answering, Benjamin ran to his room and shut the door with a loud bang. It was just not fair; life was not fair. Uncle George had just begun to help him deal with his bullies and he was leaving. Benjamin could hear chatter and laughter from his room when his father got home not too long afterwards. His father had attempted to go into his room, but the door was locked. Benjamin pretended to be asleep when his father called for him to join them at the table for dinner. He removed his hearing aid, buried his face into his pillow and lapped the edges over his ears to keep out their voices. He thought about Germany, he thought about Uncle George locking himself in a room in a strange country, he even thought about the job. He thought about many things until he dozed off. When the six a.m. alarm woke him up for school the following morning, Uncle George was gone.

The musical was only a week away and rehearsals were taking up most of the school day. It was a long day, but it was helping to take Benjamin's mind off Uncle George's departure. The students had gotten their scripts weeks earlier and were cautioned by Mrs. Kennedy to know their parts by heart. Because Benjamin was going to be speech language interpreter – which was the most important role in the entire musical as far as he was concerned – he had received the scripts of everyone so that he could practice too.

As they had done what seemed to be a thousand times before, the students took their positions on the stage and got into performance mode. Mrs. Kennedy was strolling around authoritatively with a ruler in hand, pointing out their flaws and making suggestions. It appeared as if no one was being convincing enough, as she would constantly be yelling, "Be more convincing!" There was an important scene among Elizabeth Swann, being played by Melody, Will Turner being played by Leon, and Captain Jack Sparrow, being played by Imran. In the scene, Elizabeth's obsession with pirates had led to her falling in love with both Will and Jack. She had to make the difficult decision of choosing either her original love interest, Will, or the pirate who her heart desired the most, Jack. She was running from one end of the stage to the other, crossing props of sea weeds and washed up debris to get to the ships of both men to convince them of her love.

Benjamin was noticeably standing at the far-right front of the stage, translating the speech with his hand movements when Melody suddenly stopped.

"I can't do this!" she shouted. "I don't want to seem so desperate."

"What?" questioned a puzzled Mrs. Kennedy, knitting her brows.

Melody had folded her arms across her chest and was rocking from side to side.

"I don't want to seem so desperate by trying to get the love of two men," she said.

Mrs. Kennedy pulled her glasses to the tip of her nose before looking Melody over. "When you got the script, didn't you see that this love triangle was going to be a part of your role?" asked a very annoyed Mrs. Kennedy.

Melody was staring at the floor and did not respond. In Benjamin's heart of hearts, he did not think Melody had an issue with the role, he thought it was just Melody's way of being extra. Without warning, Mrs. Kennedy pulled the whistle that was attached to a string around her neck and started blowing into it. The loud shrilling sound echoed throughout the auditorium, prompting the attention of everyone. Even with the room going silent and everyone staring in her direction, she continued to blow. Mrs. Kennedy seemed to have deserved a place in the Guinness World Records for the longest sustained whistle blow ever done by anyone. He did not know how she did it, but she held her cheeks full with air, blowing into the shiny silver device for what seemed like forever.

The music teacher Mrs. Prescott, who had just taken a short break from assisting with the rehearsals, came rushing back into the room at the prolonged sound of the whistle. She wrestled the device from Mrs. Kennedy's clenched lips and led her to a chair at the center of the room. Mrs. Kennedy's huge bosom rose and fell dramatically as she gasped for breath while trying to fit her plump body on the small wooden chair. The ceiling fans were not enough to lower her temperature, nor her temper that was radiating heat like a hot stove. Mrs. Prescott summoned Angella to fetch a small piece of cardboard laying among the props scattered on the stage to fan Mrs. Kennedy with. Even with the extra breeze, she was still panting like a lizard on a hot rock.

"I think she is having a panic attack!" exclaimed Mrs. Prescott. She sent Angella to quickly fetch the principal.

The room was so silent it felt heavy, they thought Mrs. Kennedy was dying before their very eyes. Mr. Phillips came bursting into the room with Angella breathlessly running behind him. He rushed over to where Mrs. Kennedy was sitting with Mrs. Prescott attempting to wipe small circles of sweat from her forehead and looking quite frightened herself. Without saying a word, Mr. Phillips placed a hand on Mrs. Kennedy's back and the other on her arms. He took a deep breath as if he was summoning strength to ease Mrs. Kennedy's huge frame off the chair. Mr. Phillips' body wobbled, and his folded lips widened as he attempted to pull Mrs. Kennedy off the chair. Mrs. Prescott was standing behind her with both hands on her waist providing reinforcements for the task. In a complicated set of activities, they managed to get a trembling Mrs. Kennedy off the chair and led her down to the nurse's office in slow, measured steps. Amid the chaos, Melody had sunk to the back and was twiddling her thumbs. She was feeling the weight of every unsaid word as rows of heads turned to look at her in judgment. Melody might had gone too far this time. If Mrs. Kennedy were to die, she would be at fault. Feeling the weight of what she had done, she took up her bag and ran off to the bathroom in complete humiliation. That was the last time anyone saw Melody for the rest of the day.

Mrs. Kennedy falling ill was both good and bad. It was bad because the students did not know if she would survive. It was good because Anice and Maxwell finally had an opportunity to act in their roles as director and assistant director. The students were now on their own since Mr. Gowe, who had also been assisting with the rehearsals, was absent.

"Scene one get into position," ordered Maxwell.

The scene opened with The Flying Dutchman - Davy Jones' ship - rising from the depths of the sea to attack an unsuspecting ragtag bunch of sailors. Bodies were blasted off the ship as The Flying Dutchman plundered with its unmatched missiles. And just as mysteriously as it had emerged, it retreated into the depths of the blue sea.

"Your fall does not look real enough." Maxwell was pointing at the boys with the ruler in the same way that Mrs. Kennedy had done. "A little harder!" he shouted, as bodies came tumbling off the makeshift ship and onto the hard parquet floor.

"Benny! Give us more expression!"

Maxwell had never done sign language in all his life, yet he had the audacity to be telling Benjamin to be more expressive. Benjamin felt like blasting him, but he held his tongue.

"Just shut up!" Imran shouted.

The students were all getting annoyed with him, but Imran was letting his feelings known. That still did not phase power-drunk Maxwell who continued to shout and point with the ruler. He was not giving Anice a chance. By the time they got to scene 2 to sing "I'll tell you a tale of a pirate ship that plundered and tormented the seas...", she had quietly taken a seat. And so it was for the rest of the afternoon until the students were sent back to their classes.

"The person who left a silver package for Norman on his desk, you are needed in my office."

It was Mr. Phillips' stern voice making the same request for the third time. Benjamin sat at his desk trying to seem as unconcerned as Thomas kicking his tiny legs in his perambulator. Not wanting to bring attention to himself, he sneakingly scanned the whole room, examining the faces on bent heads studying pictures of scrotums and ovaries. Everyone was working as if they had not just heard the urgent appeal over the intercom. He looked down into his book and continued to read the chapter on the reproductive system.

"If you do not come willingly, I will find you by force."

Have you ever noticed that guilt had a way of wrapping its arms around your neck and choking the life out of you? That was what was happening to Benjamin; he was struggling to breathe. The threat from Mr. Phillips had left him in a state of panic; his arms were covered in goosebumps and he was sweating bullets. The class was alerted that something was seriously wrong and had begun to get jittery. There was much chatter about what could have possibly been enclosed in the now famous package. Benjamin was awash with guilt, the evidence of which he tried to hide by chewing on a piece of gum.

Vice Principal Doyle walked in with his dog trailing him, plunging the classroom into immediate silence. The students were about to stand in acknowledgment of his presence, but he raised his hand, sending them sliding back down into their seats. He stood at attention, measuring every last one of their faces before he spoke.

"Boy eject that gum from your trap!" he shouted.

He was staring down at Benjamin like he was just convicted of a senseless crime. VP Doyle was not a tall man, but he had this military style way of speaking and carrying himself that made everyone fear him. The weight of his eyes caused Benjamin to senselessly remove the wet gum from his mouth and throw it inside his knapsack among his belongings.

"By now you all know why I am here." He paused and looked around the classroom before he continued. "I am looking for the culprit!" he shouted, emitting fine particles of saliva from his mouth.

They were always frightened by Vice Principal Doyle, but at that moment, he had them going to pieces. The classroom was so silent you would have thought it was the day of rapture. None of the students had dared to move. Even if Benjamin were to confess to the crime, VP Doyle was the last person he would be confessing to. He did not earn the nickname Doomsday Doyle for nothing and Benjamin was not ready to meet his end. He lowered his eyes to watch the faithful dog standing next to VP Doyle wagging its tail and licking its lips as if all was well. He thought that maybe the dog was not as happy as it seemed but because VP Doyle was so heartless, he had bullied the poor animal, giving it a false sense of happiness. He felt pity for the animal for having such a callous owner.

"Since none of you seem to know who the culprit is, I will not continue to waste my time," VP Doyle said.

He turned and left in his starch pressed pants which had seams up to the waist. The dog seemed to be delighted to be on this important mission with VP Doyle, its shiny brown coat sparkled in the midmorning sun as it ran behind its master, wagging its tail.

"When I picked up the bag, did anyone see me? Did anyone see me entering the classroom? Did anyone see me leave the gift on Norman's desk?" Benjamin was asking himself all these questions in his head.

He was trying to mentally retrace his steps on that fateful day when he left the gift for Norman. Streaks of water ran down his face and arms as anxiety overtook his body. He was sure that no one saw him with the silver package because he'd had the good sense of placing it in a black plastic bag. The worrying matter for him was if anyone saw him entering the classroom with the bag. He was in grade eight and Norman's class was grade ten, Benjamin had no reason to be there. VP Doyle's visit had left the class so frightened, Mrs. Frank struggled to get them to focus again on the lesson. They were not being boisterous or anything like that, but their worlds were just turned upside down by VP Doyle's strange visit. The usual spirited discussions after the readings in the Human Development and Sexual Health textbook, was today being met with lackluster feedback.

The session ended and the students carried the tense mood to the auditorium for what would have been their performance art period. Imran was telling a crowd gathered around him that the package had contained a bomb. "I even heard that it was five minutes away from being detonated when Norman opened it. If it had gone off, we all would be dead," he said.

Imran's story was met with oohs and aahs by his gullible audience. Imran had a way with words and could easily convince people of anything with his northwestern Punjabi accent, although he said he had only been to India twice for holiday. Benjamin was disappointed with how naïve his classmates were. He walked to the back of the auditorium to get away from the enquiring chatter, he could not bear to be in the same space with the idiots who were believing everything Imran was saying.

"I might be many things, but I am no killer," Benjamin was tempted to say to the crowd gathered around Imran, but he could not risk blowing his cover.

He walked away and went to sit so far away from the others that the only thing he could hear was the cling clanging of the technical team trying to arrange speakers and boxes in position. The crowd around Imran had gotten much smaller and he reserved himself to a seat on the elevated edge of the stage, swinging his legs and looking out into the distance. VP Doyle poked his round head inside the auditorium before he stepped in. The faithful dog walked in dutifully beside him. Benjamin's palms got sweaty and his pulse quickened as VP Doyle strolled from one end of the room to the other, looking here and there. Benjamin expected that at any minute he was going to point at him and lead him away to be punished in his office. Benjamin followed his unpredictable movements with his eyes, but without saying a word, VP Doyle walked out.

Benjamin was in serious trouble, but he had resigned himself to the hope that no one saw him entering Norman's classroom. He started to wonder if he could ask his mother to transfer him to a new school, or maybe he could fake terminal illness and stop attending school. He was thinking of possible solutions to his gargantuan problem and had lost touch with time and space. The pine-lemon scent of the burning Palo Santo wood, brought him back to reality. Mrs. Kennedy was walking around the room with the holy wood, sending out calming energy into the atmosphere. "Ohm, ohm, ohm," she repeated over and over, not caring for the giggles that were coming from her onlookers. Willie took up a piece of wood and proceeded to mimic the actions of Mrs. Kennedy. Willie's action prompted a chorus of laughter from his classmates as he wobbled from side to side, making small circles with his outstretched hand. He smirked and snorted but still managed to maintain a straight face walking behind a 'ohming' Mrs. Kennedy. She turned around unexpectedly and caught him red-handed imitating her movements. His eyes widened in stunned surprise and he sprinted off before the words, "You devil" could leave her lips.

The panic attack brought on by Melody was still fresh in the students' minds. They did not want to aggravate Mrs. Kennedy any further and quickly got into their positions on stage. In between shouts of "Let's do that again" or "Be more convincing", Mrs. Kennedy strutted around at the foot of the stage, using her ruler to make small taps on her leg.

Benjamin tried to push his personal problems to the back of his mind, but he could not get the image of VP Doyle from his thoughts. Mr. Phillips' voice over the intercom had frightened him but the presence of VP Doyle had left him with a permanent queasiness in his stomach. They all had heard the stories of him lifting boys off the floor, boys much bigger than he was with just one hand. Benjamin had never witnessed any of these incidents himself, but VP Doyle had that reputation around the school, and he believed them. Benjamin was so foregone in worry that his hand movements and facial expressions were not in tandem with the words of the performers.

"What are you doing Benjamin?" Mrs. Kennedy shouted. She was unfamiliar with sign language, but it did not need an expert to see that his movements were of no order.

They were about forty minutes into the rehearsal when Mr. Lewis walked in, grinning from ear to ear. The khaki outfit, wide brimmed hat, and rubber boots that he wore to tend to the garden made him look out of place inside the auditorium. The sight of him made Benjamin's heart sink. In his mind, he was thinking Mr. Lewis was sent by VP Doyle to fetch him to face the consequences of his action. Mr. Lewis went and stood at the center of the room with his hands akimbo. He was mesmerized at the forms moving about on the stage and speaking with accents he had never heard before. He raised his eyebrows and laughed loudly when Captain Jack Sparrow tried to use wit and trickery to attain his goals. He slapped his hands on his knees and bent over, letting out a howl at Sparrow's drunken swagger. Mrs. Kennedy did what no student had ever seen her do before; she looked around at Mr. Lewis, rubbed the tip of her nose and gave out the heartiest laughter. The laughter was so full it sounded like it was coming from the pits of her stomach. Tears ran down her reddened cheeks as she struggled to stand. A boy fetched her the same small wooden chair that she had sat on during her panic attack. She plopped down, still laughing and barely managing to say, "That will be all for today."

Benjamin's walk to the tree was one of self-reflection and evaluation. Never in a million years he would have thought he could experience any remorse for getting back at Norman. He liked that Norman had suffered before he discovered the prank, but Benjamin hated the feeling of being hunted down like a common criminal. He was sorry but not sorry. The tree was unoccupied, he sat down and placed his brown paper bag next to him on the sprawling root. The branches stood unmoved in the still air. He sat blankly, staring at his doomed future ahead of him. He wrestled with the thought of confessing to Lanay about what he had done.

He was so worried that he did not hear Mr. Lewis coming or the bleating of the goat. "I did not know you were so talented," Mr. Lewis said, while holding on to the rope of the tugging goat.

Benjamin was proud that Mr. Lewis thought that he was talented. He smiled and said, "I guess so." That was the humblest answer he could think of without tooting his own horn.

"It's a very nice dance you were doing," Mr. Lewis continued.

Mr. Lewis was obviously unaware of what sign language was, and Benjamin saw it as his duty to correct him.

"It is not a dance; it is a way of talking," Benjamin said.

Mr. Lewis edged closer to the tree and held his mouth ajar in surprise.

"The movements that I was making with my hands and body are a language," Benjamin said.

Mr. Lewis leaned his head to the side and used his right hand to clutch the right side of his face like he had just gotten some unbelievable news. Benjamin saw Lanay approaching from the corner of his eyes. She was walking cheerfully and swinging a bag in her left hand that was not her usual lunch bag. She got closer but became startled by the untied goat nibbling on a patch of grass close to the tree. She gave a small shriek, placed her hand over her heart and took off running. Mr. Lewis and Benjamin chuckled and called for her to stop. Realizing the fright his goat had caused, Mr. Lewis checked the time on the invisible watch on his wrist and ambled off with his animal.

"Talk to you later Benny," he said. He fetched the rope tied around the goat's neck and trudged away, pulling the animal behind him.

Lanay returned to the tree and sat down holding the brown and red paper bag. "I forgot my lunch bag and had to wait for daddy to bring me lunch," she said.

Benjamin's mouth watered as she unwrapped the double bacon cheeseburger from the shiny wrapping paper. His stomach was full from having just eaten his peanut butter and jelly sandwiches washed down with coconut water, but that did not stop him from craving for what Lanay had.

"Do you want some fries Benny?" she asked.

She was holding the pack of fries splattered with ketchup to his face. He took the oil-soaked pack and immediately started to shove bundles of warm, salty potato fries into his mouth. The taste of the fries helped to take his mind off his troubles, although temporarily. His mouth was watering for the burger that Lanay was eating bird-like. She was taking small gingerly bites from the sandwich, chewing a thousand times before swallowing.

"You may have this," she said, handing him about three-quarters of the burger and taking what little was left of the fries.

The perfectly crisp, fatty taste of the bacon exploded on his tongue. He clenched his toes, enjoying the delicious taste of the beef burger patties, pickles, onions, and lettuce of the double cheeseburger. The combination tasted like heaven between two buns. Benjamin loved burgers but on his grandmother's advice, his parents no longer bought him fast-food although there was nothing in the world that he loved more. He ate the food as if it were his last meal. In no time, it was all gone.

He licked his fingers dribbled with ranch sauce. "Geez Benny, don't eat your fingers too," Lanay said.

Benjamin laughed sheepishly, on the realization that she was watching him so closely. He wiped his mouth with napkins from the bag and then gathered all the rubbish to throw inside the bin. The glass from the green-faced silver watch on his hand was glistening in the afternoon sun, making dancing reflections on the ground as he walked to the drum. Uncle George had gifted him the watch for his thirteenth birthday and it suddenly reminded him of his uncle, which reminded him of his problem. No one except Uncle George knew of his great secret and now he was no longer there for Benjamin to tell his problems. Lanay was a great friend and had experiences of trouble with the principal, but Benjamin did not know if he could trust her with such a great secret. He let out a deep sigh before discarding the waste inside the bin, then rejoined Lanay at the tree. He sat down and began to contemplate the pros and cons of telling on himself. They were best friends in school, but he knew that he was not her only friend. What Benjamin feared the most was if he told her and she decided to tell someone else, and that someone decided to tell someone else, until word got back to the office.

"Let us practice for the sign language club," Lanay suggested as soon as he sat down.

Lanay had gotten up and was standing eagerly in front of him. A few days ago, they had gotten up to the letter T, but he was not in the mood to teach her anything today. She sensed that he was unwilling and began to press him for his participation.

"Not today," he said.

"But why not Bennnnnnnyyyyyy?" she asked.

She was tilting her head to the side and pulling his right arm. He pulled back and she eventually released her grasp. She sat down again and began biting down on her lip.

"I did it Lanay," he said.

She knew immediately what he was talking about. She looked over at him with wide opened eyes. "You mean VP Doyle?" she asked. He barely nodded before she burst out laughing.

"Benny you are a hero."

She was on the ground cackling and tears were streaming down her face.

The auditorium was alive with chatter when Mr. Phillips walked on stage with a dejected looking Norman taking stealthy steps behind him. He stood slump-shouldered with his head bent and both hands fumbling in his pockets. For the first time in his life, Norman was not on the stage because he was in trouble. Benjamin was overtaken with worry, but he managed to collect himself and stared poker-faced at the proceedings. Resounding sounds of "shhhh" travelled throughout the auditorium as Mr. Phillips reached forward and took up the microphone.

"By now, you all must have heard what has happened to Norman."

Norman raised his head at the sound of his name but quickly lowered it again.

"A very unconscionable person preyed on his inability to smell and had him walking around smelling like a pigsty for weeks."

Mr. Phillips eased his body forward by standing on his tiptoes and raised his voice to enunciate the last two words in the sentence. Someone at the back gave a mocking "oink oink", causing some students to chuckle. Mr. Phillips was not amused and gave the crowd a harsh stare. His displeasure prompted the teachers to abandon their relaxed positions at the sides of the room and begin patrolling the lines targeting chatterboxes. They could tell Norman was very embarrassed to be compared to a pigsty. He stood uneasily on the stage, moving his body weight from one leg to the other. If it were another person, Benjamin might have felt pity, but it was Norman, and he was his enemy.

"In the spirit of the school community, you all have a responsibility to be kind to everyone. You should never do such wickedness to a fellow schoolmate. It is very distasteful to prey on the weakness of another." Mr. Phillips stopped speaking and used his free hand to scratch the back of his head before he continued.

"The aim of the school is to produce selfless citizens whose duty it is to make the world a better place for everyone." He was speaking in his usual slow, monotonous way which was causing Benjamin's anxiety to increase.

During Mr. Phillips' speech, Lanay's eyes found Benjamin's and she gave him a quick smile. He did not smile back; he had no intention of blowing his cover. His refusal to acknowledge her prompted her to start waving wildly and grinning her teeth. He sighed and turned his back to where she was standing in line, regretting his stupid decision to tell her about his secret. As Mr. Phillips spoke, Benjamin was a combination of guilt and fright, but he reasoned that his secret would always be safe as long as Lanay kept her mouth shut.

"The guilty party please let yourself known," Mr. Phillips demanded.

He had moved from behind the lectern and was standing at the front of the stage, tapping the tip of his left shoe on the floor. The auditorium went silent as if they were expecting a dark figure to emerge from the shadows confessing to their sins. Norman was still standing in place with his head bent.

"There are more ways of killing a cat than by choking it with cream," Mr. Phillips said in a slow matter-of-fact manner after a few minutes with no movement.

He stopped speaking and pointed to the cameras hanging from the ceiling of the auditorium. Benjamin was immediately casted into a state of intolerable discomfort. His stomach rumbled and he had a strong desire to use the toilet. He knew his time as an outlaw was about to come to an end; there was absolutely no way he was going to get out of this. He looked over at Lanay who was staring at him with her mouth opened wide. His legs had turned to jelly, and it felt almost impossible for him to stand for much longer.

But the last thing either Lanay or Benjamin was expecting happened. A grade eleven boy broke away from the crowd and ran onto the stage shouting, "I did it! I did it!" The auditorium took a collective breath as the boy collapsed at the feet of the principal in tears. His glasses fell from his face and he used the back of his hand to wipe his narrow, slanted eyes. It took a few seconds for Mr. Phillips to grasp what was happening. He held the scrawny looking boy by his wrist and roughly pulled him to his feet. Benjamin could feel Lanay's eyes focused on him, but he held his head down, examining his dirty shoes that he had forgotten to polish the night before. It was the last thing either of them was expecting; it was as if they just had a sighting of the Loch Ness Monster. During the excitement, VP Doyle took the microphone and shooed the students off to their classes. Benjamin evaded Lanay and walked to his destination alone. Swarms of clueless students walked up the staircase and into their classrooms abuzz with chatter, making assumptions.

When he got to class, Mrs. Vassell was already there looking like Big Bird. She was wearing a bright yellow skirt suit, red sheer stockings and red shoes. She was placing papers facedown on the desks with the usual evil smirk on her face. Benjamin slowly pulled the chair from under the table, and the iron legs made a screeching sound as they were drawn over the surface of the concrete floor. Mrs. Vassell turned her head towards where he was standing, looked him over like a dirty rag, then placed one finger over her thin lips and said, "Shhhh" in the most irritated way.

Benjamin took his seat quietly and waited for her instructions concerning the paper laying on his desk. Willie and Leon were fussing at the back over whose turn it was to sit on the padded chair. He turned around to observe what was happening and saw that Mrs. Vassell's attention was totally focused on the two boys. Everyone else's heads were turned towards the squabble, or they were frantically digging into their knapsacks trying to find pens or erasers. Benjamin used the opportunity to quickly flip over the paper, disregarding the boldly written Do Not Turnover instruction on the back. It was an impromptu test on the story *The Necklace*. The class had not too long ago completed the story and he had remembered that the message was about being satisfied with what one had. He did not remember much else and would have failed if he did not act fast. Benjamin thought that he was already about to be in trouble with the school, he could not risk failing his English literature test again. He made a quick mental note of the ten questions before turning over the paper and contemplating his next move. Mrs. Vassell had moved away from the boys and was now standing at Melody's desk, watching over her as she removed the forbidden silver hoop earrings from her ears. Benjamin reached inside his knapsack, removed the storybook, discreetly placed it inside his shirt and lapped it under his arm.

"Mrs. Vassell, I really need to use the bathroom," Benjamin said.

He was standing up and was twisting and turning his legs, putting on his best Oscar performance.

"You have five minutes to get back," Mrs. Vassell said, eyeing the big clock at the front of the room.

He pretended to be holding his stomach and rushed from the class and down the hallway to the bathroom.

It took Benjamin more than five minutes to get back from his mission. The other students were already working on their tests when he slipped in and sat at his desk, careful not to cause any disturbance with his chair. Richard was blankly staring into nothingness as if he had given up all hope on answering any of the questions correctly. Benjamin turned over the paper and held his face in a way as if he was seeing the questions for the first time. Mrs. Vassell was weaving through rows of desks and chairs, the ever-present smirk plastered on her face. Benjamin breezed through the questions, answering each one with little thought. He was a novice to cheating and had not paced himself to give his dishonesty a hint of believability. He completed the test too quickly and was idly tapping his pen on the table causing Mrs. Vassell to approach his desk and take up his paper.

She silently examined his answers, looking from the paper to Benjamin, and from Benjamin to the paper. She was looking as if she was not convinced about what her eyes were seeing. Benjamin was overtaken with worry and tried to keep his eyes averted as she looked over his answers. He could not keep his eyes averted for long because his nervousness kept on forcing him to examine the expression on Mrs. Vassell's face. The deep lines in her forehead covered by layers of makeup were becoming more noticeable as she read through his paper. Mrs. Vassell was puzzled, it was like a miracle was happening before her eyes, but unbeknownst to her, Benjamin had outsmarted her. Silent triumph overtook him when she placed the paper on his desk and strolled off. He had cheated but he felt the absence of shame. As far as he was concerned, it was Mrs. Vassell's own fault which had forced him to cheat. All teachers knew that he had a special need and should be given differentiated tests and exams. Mrs. Vassell was a spiteful woman who thought she was above the orders of the Ministry of Education. Benjamin believed that she was cheating as much as he was.

His instinct told him to try and look less idle. He lowered his head to read and re-read the questions and his written rehearsed answers for about a dozen times. He could feel Mrs. Vassell's bulging eyes piercing through his bent head, but he kept his cool. Even if she had demanded to search him, there would be no evidence of his cheating. There were no scribbles in his hand, nor book on his person. Benjamin used his pen to dot a few I's and cross a few T's, presenting himself as the ardent literature student he was not.

The auditorium confession was still weighing heavily on his mind. What had motivated the boy to confess was outside the realm of Benjamin's understanding. He thought that maybe the boy was afflicted with a dash of insanity which had caused him to take on his problems. Benjamin's discomfort and confusion felt like a muddy pit he was slowly drowning in. He wanted to be happy, but he feared being premature in his celebrations.

"You are out of time everyone." Mrs. Vassell's tone had hardened, and she was moving from table to table yanking papers from beneath jittery pens.

She roughly gathered the last of the papers and flounced from the classroom. Students immediately huddled, anxiously comparing their answers and consulting Florence or their texts for confirmation. Ms. Samuels came in and the students took their seats. Benjamin was in the mood for one of her travel stories, but she was not in the mood to thrill them. She wrote some math problems on the whiteboard and silently took her seat at her desk. There was just something about Ms. Samuels' behavior that laid heavily on his heart. Sometimes after school, she would sit alone in Mr. Lewis' garden and look longingly at students walking past with their futures ahead.

The afternoon was ablaze with the Caribbean sun when Benjamin left the class for the tree. Lanay's head bobbled in the lunchtime crowd headed for the outdoors or the canteen. He peeled through the crowd to catch up with her as she was exiting the main door. She was wearing her hair a different way today; it was a cornrow style with zig-zag parts making their way from her forehead to the nape of her neck. He stretched his hand across her slender frame to her right shoulder and gently tapped it. She did not fall for his trick and looked over to her left shoulder as he was about to innocently look away.

"Benny you play too much." She laughed, slapping the back of his head with her small hand.

He became temporarily blinded by the bright rays when they exited the building. He held his hand over his eyes to block the direct glimmer of sunlight. Lanay slightly nudged his side with her elbow and used her lips to point to Norman who was walking just a few feet away with Buster and a few others. Norman had not only regained his sense of smell, but he had also regained his following. Their closeness in proximity to Norman highlighted the horrible condition of his head and how tattered his uniform was. The sighting of Norman made Lanay eager to talk about what had happened in the auditorium, but he cautioned her against doing so before they got to the tree. Plus, he was going to take her to task for waving at him in the auditorium like she did not have an ounce of common sense.

They walked in silence, trailing slowly behind a once again discourteous Norman and his henchmen. Lanay kept her eyes on Norman and was still using her lips to point at the pus-filled fungus in the back of his head. She flashed her fingers and then used them to muffle the laughter coming from her mouth. Benjamin remained quiet, although he was irritated with her for not knowing when to take things seriously. He stopped with her along the foot-beaten track and watched as she removed a banana peel from her lunch bag, which she threw to the goat. Her irrational fear of the animal had not diminished, but she was comfortable with it as long as it remained tied to the shrub. They took a second to watch the goat eat the peel like it was a five-star restaurant delicacy. Benjamin's eyes drifted to the flower garden where a clutch of bird eggs was nestled deeply in the garden poinsettias. It immediately crossed his mind that he and the eggs were somewhat in the same predicament; their futures were dependent on no one discovering their secrets.

"Last person to get to the tree smells like Norman!" Lanay shouted and took off running. Her skinny legs looked like drumsticks going down the red-dirt slope to the tree.

Benjamin thought it was pointless to run after her although he knew he could outrun her if he really wanted to. His mother had packed a slice of cherry-flavored cheesecake for him in his paper bag and he did not want to ruin it by running and shaking it too roughly. She was grinning widely when he set his paper bag down and took a seat beside her in the shade of the tree. He allowed her to revel in the glory of her triumph without interruption. Lanay was upbeat and chatty and wanted to talk about everything. She spoke of the musical – not critically – she was contented in her role wearing a tree costume forming a part of the jungle. It was not what he was expecting but by now he had come to accept the complexity of her character.

The thick sauce from the stewed peas was curdled over the rice when he opened the Tupperware containing his lunch. Lanay took a break from talking and licked her lips at the sight of the chunks of salted beef. He handed her the container in exchange for her foil-wrapped full-house sandwiches. She instantly shoved big spoonfuls of the cold rice and stewed peas into her small mouth. He took a bite from one of the sandwiches; the toasted bread was crispy, just the way he liked it.

"Thanks for grinning and waving at me like you are a baboon, this morning," Benjamin said after he had swallowed the piece of sandwich he had bitten off.

"It was a pleasure," Lanay responded, although she had recognized the sarcasm in his statement.

There was nothing funny about what he had said but she placed the dish on the tree and started hopping around like a monkey. She screeched "eech eech", slapping her hands on her thighs and grinning her teeth. It was a serious matter, and he became annoyed with her for taking it so lightly.

"You bloody idiot!" he shouted.

Benjamin immediately regretted his decision to use such hateful words. The words incited a firestorm in her and she did not spare his feelings when unleashing her rage.

"I am an idiot? You let Norman beat your behind in front of the whole school and you barely did anything about it."

She sat down again and was biting down on her lip. She pushed the Tupperware to the side and did not continue eating the food. Benjamin was seething with anger. He could not understand why she would use his Achilles heel to get back at him. Deep down he knew he was wrong for calling her an idiot, he had allowed his emotions to take over his head. But he believed that she was wrong too, she knew how much Norman had terrorized him and how much he hated Norman for it. The two of them sat in uncomfortable silence, Lanay not eating, but Benjamin continued eating the full-house sandwiches in flavorless spit-filled bites.

He wanted to talk to her, but he held back for as long as he could until he could hold it no more.

"Do you want some cake?" He held out the container bearing the nicely sized cake in front of her face. He knew that of course, she wanted it, she loved pastry even more than he did. She took the container from his hand without verbally responding to his question. Using the fork to scoop the cake out of the container, in one massive bite, she took off more than half. Her cake-filled cheeks made her look like a squirrel collecting nuts for winter. In a fit of panic, Benjamin grabbed the remaining cake from her hand. Her body trembled with laughter as she struggled to chew the contents of her full mouth.

The next day seemed to get stranger by the minute. Firstly, the scrawny looking boy was still accepting responsibility for Benjamin's crime. He approached the auditorium stage sullen-looking and downcasted. His pants were about three sizes too large and swung like a hoisted flag around his skinny legs as he walked. He took the microphone and spoke feebly into it.

"I want to apologize to Norman and the school for the embarrassment I have caused. I might have taken my experiment for the grade eleven science competition a little too far. I was trying to prove the hypotheses that our sense of smell is important for our survival. I am sorry for using Norman as my guinea pig to test my hypotheses. If it is not too much to ask, I am hoping he will avail himself for a follow-up interview with me. Despite my mistake, I hope that my entry will still be considered by the judges since I have met the criteria of being creative with a clear and focused purpose." He adjusted the thick glasses on his face and placed the microphone on the lectern. He folded the piece of paper he had delivered the message from, and modestly walked off the stage. His jet-black hair bounced on his head as he made his way to join his class line.

Benjamin could not believe his ears; this boy was a genius. He had managed to fool everyone in the school except Lanay and Benjamin. The possibility of winning a spanking new bicycle with a matching helmet had circumvented any fear he had of getting in trouble. It was clear that winning was the most important thing in this boy's life; it was even more important than the possibility of being suspended.

The school was bustling with chatter at the end of devotion. Everyone was talking about the boy and how clever he was. Benjamin's grade remained in the auditorium for the final fittings of their costumes for the musical. Tomorrow was going to be the big day, and they still had a lot to be done. There was a loud thud and he turned around to see tardy Lanay struggling to pick up a thick book which had fallen. She unsteadily balanced the book beneath her arm and ran off with a myriad of other things in her hands, trying to catch up with her classmates who were headed to the audio-visual room for their final fittings. Her oversized bag gave the illusion of pulling her over as it bounced about on her narrow back.

A tall woman came sauntering in carrying numerous bags of costumes. She set them down untidily on the stage and left in a rush. Her high heels clicked against the tiles and her legs wiggled in the brown pointed-toe shoes as she hurried from the auditorium. She returned shortly after carrying more bags which she tossed onto the stage in the same haphazard manner before leaving again. She did this maybe four or five times, glistening brighter each time she returned from walking in the morning sun.

Piles of woolen breeches, multi-colored linen shirts, cotton waistcoats, knitted caps, bandanas and stockings, flowed from the bags and onto the floor. The woman was still busy but this time she was transporting bags of costumes up the stairs to the audio-visual room. Mrs. Kennedy had not arrived as yet, and the students were growing impatient. Melody took it up on herself to rescue her classmates from their state of restlessness and started doing eye measurements between clothes and body sizes. Her estimated measurements were followed by her rummaging through bags and issuing out costumes. Excited students rushed off to the restrooms in the back, returning shortly after dressed as pirates. Because Benjamin thought he was the unluckiest person in the world, and he did not foresee a positive outcome to this scheme, he found a chair and sat detached from the happenings.

Dino came staggering from the back with a heavily soiled shirt stuck to his portly torso. Layers of fat folded under the sleeves of the sweat-soaked shirt. His stomach fat jiggled beneath the unbuttoned garment as he walked to the stage appealing for help. Every thread of the linen material was struggling to keep the garment intact. It was a sight to behold as he twisted and turned his huge frame, trying to get out of the entrapment he was in. The shirt would not budge, it was as if it was glued to his skin. Melody knew that this was her fault and attempted to help. She had worked out a plan to carefully peel the garment off him rather than pulling it. Dino stuck his right hand out to the side and Melody tried to release him by slowly rolling the garment off his shoulder and down his plump arms.

They were not achieving the results they were hoping for. Dino's arm became stuck in an uncomfortable position, causing him to stand on his tiptoes and yelp "ouch, ouch, ouch" as he wiggled his big body. He held his face in a grimace and was squealing like his body was being hung over a torturous pyre. Melody was taken aback by his reaction and immediately withdrew her plan.

The remaining contents of the bags had warranted the full attention of everyone else in the room who were busy matching bandanas, hats, eye-patches and knitted caps with their outfits. They fit the image of a motley crew of sailors strolling around in their too tight, too loose, too big, too small, or too tall costumes. Benjamin sat and watched as pockets of spectacle unfolded before him. A struggling Dino remained bounded in his entrapment with no help from a sulking Melody who had retreated to the back of the room.

Mrs. Kennedy arrived bright-eyed and alarmed. She blew her whistle, garnering the attention of the ill-fated pirates who were nonchalantly strolling around. The glee in their mood was instantly drained away by her admonishment of them for their forwardness. Alarmed by her reaction, bodies were scampering everywhere, hastily removing the costumes and replacing them with their uniforms. Dino must have thought he would have to spend the rest of his days in a pirate's shirt and started to cry loudly. The auditorium became focused on Dino who had tears streaming down his round cheeks. In between sobs, he said something about being unable to move his hands which made everyone assume the shirt was so tight, it was cutting off the blood circulation in his arms.

"How will I eat if I can't move my hands?" he cried more clearly.

Mrs. Kennedy placed both hands on her head and stood staring at Dino in astonishment. Willie thought that he should add to Dino's dismay. He removed a bar of chocolate from his pocket and unwrapped it, revealing its rich dark, nutty texture. He passed it slowly beneath Dino's nose and then bit down into the bar in slow mocking motions. This caused Dino to become crazy like a rabid dog. He twisted his body and in one big movement, there was an extended screech coming from the shirt. The shirt had split evenly down the back and had thread fraying everywhere.

"My Jesus, Mary and Moses!" shouted a stunned Mrs. Kennedy.

Dino tore off the remains of the shirt still hanging from his body and threw them onto the floor. He rushed off to the bathroom, feeling ashamed about what had happened. There would be no time to make a new shirt, the show was tomorrow, and Mrs. Kennedy was in a quandary. She walked from one end of the room to the other, with both hands still on her head, doing a low prolonged moan. Melody remained seated at the back of the room, distancing herself from everything that was happening.

The costume lady returned to the chaos in the auditorium. Bits and pieces of costumes were littered all over the floor, causing her to stand frozen with her mouth wide open. She had replaced her high heels with a more convenient pink furry sandal. She used a white handkerchief with embroidered patterns to wipe her sweating brows, transferring brown makeup from her face to the cloth. An embarrassed Mrs. Kennedy approached her, begging pardon for the teenaged enthusiasm that was responsible for the disorder. The woman was clearly in no mood for whatever excuse Mrs. Kennedy was coming with; she simply ignored her and ran fervently to the bags. Just as she had planned, each bag had a number to match with the students' names and sizes that were neatly typed on the papers she was holding in her hands. Unfortunately, there were no costumes to match them with; the bags were empty.

"Who did this?" she asked through clenched teeth.

The skin around her eyes tightened and the once unseen vein in her forehead started to throb. The students were too frightened to answer. She placed her hands on her hips and looked around at the mess scattered about. She was wearing too much lipstick on her lips, causing the intense colour of the Russian red to transfer to her teeth. The stain on her teeth made her look like she had just devoured uncooked meat, the thought of which sent a chill down Benjamin's spine. There was a long pause with no movement which made it seem as if they were frozen in time. She gave them a look of contempt and irritation before storming from the room. Without looking back, she threw the pieces of paper with the students' names and sizes in the air and disappeared down the corridor. Nothing good could come of her departure and Mrs. Kennedy knew this.

"All of you will be punished for this."

Mrs. Kennedy threateningly shook her index finger before she turned around to chase the woman. The absence of sound consumed the room. They watched with knots in their throats as Mrs. Kennedy panted heavily, pulled the hem of her skirt above her chunky knees and sprinted from the room. On her way through the door, she bumped into Mrs. Vassell who was entering the auditorium with her class register in hand.

"Howdy Kelly," Mrs. Vassell said, pausing as if she was expecting polite talk.

Mrs. Kennedy barely muttered something back at her while continuing her quest to retrieve the costume designer. She had no time for niceties as she ran down the corridor in the same direction of the costume lady, with her hands still holding up her skirt. The students were enveloped in a lull when Mrs. Vassell's tall, stick-figure frame came parading through the room.

"What is happening here?" Mrs. Vassell asked, pointing to the disarray.

She did not wait for an answer. She immediately ordered everyone to pick up the costumes strewn about the floor. Students were looking from one to the other suspiciously, behaving as if making the first move was an admission of guilt. The distrust had left everyone immobile until the threat of losing points from their final grades were given. There was immediate movement. Ex-pirates were dutifully picking up items of clothing from the floor and stuffing them into bags. Benjamin remained seated on the chair, quietly observing every flaw on Mrs. Vassell's face and thinking how agonizing she was.

"No, no, no, not like that. You have to fold them neatly before placing them inside the bags!" Mrs. Vassell shouted.

It was not her business, but as usual Mrs. Vassell was making the students' transgressions her business and was belting out orders. Benjamin thought that maybe if she paid a little attention to her own business, she would have noticed that her outdated jherri-curl hair was leaving a discolored wet line on her shirt collar.

"Benjamin Morgan, you have to get up and help," she said.

He was hoping to go unnoticed and had his head hidden behind a book. He was seated on a chair and did not see any reason to help with something he had not done. Unsurprisingly, Mrs. Vassell's binocular-sized eyes had found him. He was tempted to protest, an act that was outside his reputation and the expectations of his parents. The look on his face was perhaps very telling, causing her to justify her demand.

"You were in the room while it was happening and did nothing to stop it."

Mrs. Vassell had walked over to where Benjamin was sitting and was staring down at him. Her warm breath smelled of the early morning omelets and vanilla-flavoured Nescafé the canteen served to teachers. He told himself that it was not worth arguing and getting a detention over something as minor as stuffing some clothes into a bag. He exhaled loudly and eased his body up off the chair. Benjamin was walking away when she placed her hands on his shoulders, stopping him.

"You have both hearing aids again," Mrs. Vassell said, looking him over.

"Yes ma'am," he said in response to the obvious.

Yesterday after school his mother had driven him to Mr. Farad's office. The hearing aid had arrived earlier than expected and was just in time for the show. Mr. Farad, in his detailed way of doing things, had insisted that he conduct another audiometry test on Benjamin's hearing so that he could fine-tune the amplification levels on his hearing aid. The audiometry test was a very simple procedure. Mr. Farad gave him a pair of headphones to wear and made him listen to various tones at different pitches and volumes into one ear at a time. His mother had to leave the room with babbling Thomas because there should not even be the slightest sound while Benjamin was being tested. He had done this test numerous times before and he lingered on the edge of boredom. Benjamin was tired of raising his left hand or his right hand to indicate when he was hearing a sound in each ear. Mr. Farad knew he was done when he dozed off.

No one else had noticed that Benjamin was wearing both devices and he was surprised that Mrs. Vassell had noticed. He walked to the stage and picked up the bag which had the letter B attached to it. Richard went over and used his big athletic hands to press down against the piles of clothes that were stocked in the bag. They did this with all the other bags before neatly leaning them upward against the wall. The ripped shirt was picked up off the floor and placed in the garbage bin behind the stage.

Mrs. Kennedy was taking forever to return, and the students were on their own. Mrs. Vassell had marked the register with the names of the students who would have been present in her class and left. Melody had attracted a small crowd of impressionable girls who watched in amazement as she undid her plaits, revealing waves of hair flowing over her shoulders. She often credited her hair length and cornmeal-coloured skin to her grandfather's father being Lebanese. Benjamin thought it was just something else for her to boast about. She swung her head from left to right, causing the thick tresses to lift off her shoulders and swing in the open air. Angella was inspired by Melody's display and undid her own hair. Her coily hair did not flow down but stood stubbornly in defiance of gravity. Angella's hair in an afro magnificently accentuated her straight face, she looked like the Egyptian queen Nefertiti, whose tomb Ms. Samuels said she had visited. Her hair worn like that permanently would probably let Benjamin forget how bland she was.

Mrs. Kennedy returned to the auditorium immersed in light-hearted conversation with the costume lady. They were walking side by side and were talking about things that were causing them to laugh. None of the students were expecting this bonding of the two and they were mindful of doing anything that could jeopardize this state of happiness. The restored order of the bags left a calm air over the room. It made the costume lady friendly, a state she remained in for the rest of the day. Someone had had the good sense to retrieve the papers and place them on top of the bags from which she matched names and sizes to the small tags bearing numbers sewn onto the insides of the costumes. There was a shirt missing for Leon, which the costume lady said she might have miscounted and would have to sew that night. No one told her about the incident with Dino.

CHAPTER

16

We were always just one event away from our lives being torn apart. Not that his life was torn apart forever, but Benjamin felt worthless. He felt his birth was perhaps a mistake. It was supposed to be one of the highest points in his life; a day where he would show the world that he could do what the rest of the school could not. He was accustomed to being reduced to his inability to hear, but on that day, Norman somehow managed to move him rapidly from a state of happiness to hopelessness. Benjamin was perfectly pleased with himself at one moment and overcome with grief the next. Maybe at another time and on another day, Norman's remark would not have made such an impression on him. He would have seen this encounter as unimportant if Norman had not laughed and reduced him to a dumb boy.

"Dumb boy, you can hear again," Norman snickered.

Norman was pointing at Benjamin's hearing aids when they met on the staircase on Benjamin's way to the audio-visual room. He had not spoken to Lanay in two days and wanted to see how she was doing and also get a look at their set design for the show. She had told him that the stage design was like a real jungle, but Benjamin wanted to see it for himself.

He became unsettled by Norman's comment. He was about to embark on the most important mission of his life and Norman had cruelly stripped him of his elation. The sadness filled every cell of Benjamin's body, causing him to terminate his mission to visit Lanay. He returned to the auditorium where too much was taking place. The costume lady was there with another woman and they were busy making final adjustments to outfits. Mrs. Kennedy was going over the script with Patrick, whose nerves were causing him to stutter and jumble his lines. The sound crew was trying to find out the cause of the frying noise coming from the speakers. Benjamin's mother and a few other parents had volunteered to help with the set design and they were wrestling with yards of sky-blue fabric they were gluing to the wall. There was a trail of sand leading from the outdoors to the stage which was causing people to skid as they walked. Mr. Lewis was trying to remove the sand from the floor by using a broom with an exceptionally long handle, which made it better suited to remove cobwebs from the ceilings. The repetitive hammering from Mr. Gowe and his crew attaching sails and anchors to the ships was driving Benjamin up the wall. He wandered close to where his mother and rest of the volunteers were working, and she saw him.

"Benny come and help me with this," his mother called.

She was struggling to maneuver the slippery silk fabric and the glue gun at the same time. Benjamin took the glue gun and made huge squirts of the hot liquid onto the wall. His mother would immediately press the cloth down onto the liquid, sometimes burning the tips of her fingers.

"What's wrong Benny?" she asked.

The sadness was so profound on his face, he could not hide it. His mother could always detect when something was off with his mood, even when he tried. Benjamin was thankful that his mother had detected only sadness and not the rage he held for Norman. It was a horrible thing to withhold from his parents, but he did not want to worry them with things he should be able to deal with on his own. Plus, he did not want them to feel as if they were failing him in any way.

"I am just hungry," Benjamin said.

"Sit there and eat your orange."

His mother was pointing to a clear spot on the stage where a small backless chair rested against the bare wall. He took the orange from his lunch bag and ate in such a way that prevented the juices from spilling over to the floor. Florence's mother now had the glue gun and Benjamin watched as she and his mother worked in rhythmic motions, spraying the glue and then attaching the fabric to the wall. They were working their way closer to where Benjamin was sitting with his orange in one hand, and puzzle book in the other. Because Mr. Farad had fine-tuned the amplification levels on his hearing aid, Benjamin's hearing was even clearer now. He overheard Florence's mother expressing pity for Ms. Samuels who never seemed to have recovered from having been jilted at the altar by a man who went on to marry another woman shortly after. This was adult conversation, and Benjamin did not want his mother to know that he was eavesdropping. He bent his head looking into his puzzle book, pretending not to hear a word of what was being said.

Amidst the hustle and bustle, a man came into the auditorium carrying a tripod stand, two cameras of different sizes attached to strings around his neck, and a cross body bag swung over his shoulder. He was complaining loudly about being paid only half of the cost for his service before the show. Mrs. Kennedy raised her head long enough to give him a cutting stare before resuming her work with Patrick. The cameraman fussed for about ten minutes until he realized that his murmurs were not receiving the traction he was hoping for and he went quiet.

Mr. Lewis and Fin-Hand were methodically lining up metal chairs in rows inside the auditorium. The room was separated into halves, each side having about fifteen chairs in a row, with a space down the middle to walk. There were padded chairs at the front with VIP taped onto the seats which were reserved for important people. The auditorium looked fancy with the potted poinsettia and red ginger lily plants adding vibrant colour to the decor.

Benjamin had driven past the van with the school's logo parked at the House-of-Flowers when his mother was dropping him off at school in the morning.

Light raindrops patted their faces as Benjamin and his mother left the auditorium to go home and return in time for the 6 p.m. show. His mother had parked the car at the northern end of the building; a place reserved for teachers and visitors alike. On the way home, they stopped by the crèche to collect Thomas who was fast asleep when his mother brought him to the car and strapped him into his seat. Benjamin tickled his nose and giggled when Thomas smacked his hand in annoyance before going right back to sleep. Benjamin's grandparents were waiting for them at home when they got there. His grandparents met them at the car when his mother drove into the garage. His grandmother almost had to stand on her toes to kiss his forehead and rub his head in her usual way when he stepped from the car. She looked beautiful dressed in a knee-length white linen dress with white cut-away sandals. Her tapered pixie haircut with patches of silver hair added to her ageless appearance.

They ate a simple dinner of rice and fricassee chicken. His grandmother was on a strict Mediterranean diet and elected to have fresh vegetables with cubes of goat's cheese, sprinkled with a spoonful of extra virgin olive oil. The mood was light with no need for formalities, so they sat wherever they were most comfortable. His mother and grandfather sat at the kitchen counter and mostly ate in silence. Benjamin loved to watch Thomas whenever he ate, he sat on the floor with his plate on a tray in his lap across from Thomas in the living room. Thomas had begun to partake in meals from the family pot and had emptied the contents of his dish and cup on to his highchair. He used his hands to scoop juice-dripping rice and chicken into his mouth. His grandmother sat at the dining room table where she chewed her salad with the grace of a queen.

Benjamin checked his cellphone before going to the bathroom. He had received a good luck video message from Winter who had made a banner with his name in bold sparkly letters. She was smiling wider than usual, revealing braces on her straight teeth. Benjamin was still adjusting to how new she had become. Even from the video, it was obvious that Winter had lost a little weight from her already thin frame. Her sometimes coily, sometimes straightened hair had highlighted streaks of colour, which she changed often. Benjamin noticed that she had gained a certain brightness and confidence which was present in her Instagram photos. She would pose in the pictures with slight bends in the elbows or knees with the weight of her body on one leg, her shoulder would be facing one way and her head in another. Winter's growing internet popularity had gained her a notable number of followers who were swift to like and comment on her signature arched back, chest pushed out images. Benjamin sent her a quick thank you video message and returned his phone to his bedside drawer for use over the weekend.

Benjamin's father was busy but had made the effort to get home early. Since starting his own accounting firm, he had been extra busy with things that new business owners do. Things like registering the business name, finding a web page designer, applying for licenses, renting office space, and a whole host of other things. Benjamin was happy that his father had come home early, but he hoped that the musical was not an inconvenience for him.

"Where is my superstar son?" his father called as he came through the door.

Benjamin had talked himself into a state of tranquility, but the importance his family was placing on the show was making him nervous. His grandmother was helping him to run his belt through the back loops of his pants which he had missed earlier. Benjamin's grandmother smiled, making a deep upward curve on her lips at the sound of her son's voice.

"He is in here, Lennox," she called to her son from Benjamin's room.

Benjamin's father came and leaned against his door jamb. He had his arms folded across his chest and was smiling at Benjamin like he had just won a gold medal. He watched as his mother fussed over Benjamin's appearance and asked for what seemed like the tenth time that afternoon if he felt fine, to which he nodded.

"Are you ready?" his father asked, uncrossing his arms and placing them in his pants pockets.

"My boy is almost ready," his grandmother responded as she placed her index finger on her tongue and used the wet finger to wipe the corners of his eyes. She took his hearing aids and replenished the devices with new batteries although they still had about four days before the batteries would go dead.

Before he left, his grandmother called for everyone to gather in a circle in the living room. The family held hands and she prayed a prayer of success over the show. His mother made him repeat his affirmation for the day before leaving with his father.

His father dropped him off at school an hour before guests were scheduled to arrive. A cluster of students were already gathered in the auditorium tying bandanas around their heads and pasting patches over their eyes. The make-up team was applying scars and bruises onto the faces and bodies of the scroungy looking pirates. Benjamin waved at Patrick who was sitting and shaking his legs on one of the VIP padded chairs. He looked like the bona fide Davy Jones, with locks of hair representing tentacles hanging from his face. Patrick waved back at Benjamin, his hand held rigidly with fingers unmoving, displaying black polished nails. Imran was strutting around in his Captain Jack Sparrow garb; his blond locked wig held down by a red bandana contributed to his haphazard and thoughtless sense of style. The layers of scarves, belts, waist coats, boots, multiple cardigans and a sword holster made Imran look as crazy as the character he was going to be playing. Benjamin was waiting in line to get a black line drawn under his right eye by the make-up team when Melody came in wearing a red 18th century dress accentuated by a black corset, and walked straight to the front of the line. She shook her head in objection when she was told to wait behind the cast members who had joined the line before her arrival. The make-up team ignored Melody's claim to privilege because she was the main actress. She stood defiantly to the side of the line complaining until Mrs. Kennedy came and blew the whistle in her ears. She unwillingly trudged to the back of the line, sulking.

The cameraman was still in the auditorium and had hoisted a digital video camera on to the tripod stand, which he swiveled from one end to the other to test its accuracy. Another boy, who was about Benjamin's age, was with him and was holding one of the smaller cameras he had around his neck earlier. They were walking around capturing candid images of the students getting ready for the show. The cast members sometimes gathered in groups to do silly poses or funny facial expressions for the cameras.

The heavy curtains were drawn, concealing the cast members as respectably dressed people came filing into the auditorium. Mrs. Kennedy was in a corner talking Patrick down from an anxiety attack. Patrick was slowly sipping on a cup of water which was in danger of spilling due to the tremors of his body. Benjamin poked his head from behind the curtain just in time to see his family along with Oliver and his mother, arrive and take their seats at the right side of the room. He would be doing his performance from the left side of the stage and would have preferred if they had sat on that side of the auditorium. He pushed his hand and head from behind the curtain and was waving wildly to get their attention, but they did not see him.

Maybe it was his imagination, but Benjamin was almost sure that he could hear a chorus of hearts palpitating against the chests of the soon to be performers backstage. The auditorium was almost at capacity and it was getting harder for Benjamin to control his nerves. He melted into the corner with his back rubbing against the blue silk fabric and repeated one of his mother's affirmation that she had pasted onto his bedroom wall.

"I am capable and successful in everything I do," Benjamin whispered.

He repeated the statement several times until his hands felt a little less clammy. The sound of the students breathing was the only noise coming from the back of the stage. Leon took off his pirate's hat and started to rotate it on his forefinger. Imran was sitting on one of the prop treasure chests and was digging for his own treasure from his nose. Other students had resorted to their own type of habits or activities to settle their nerves.

"Get into position everyone!"

The serious tone of Mrs. Kennedy's voice sent Benjamin's heart plunging from his chest. The room had suddenly become too cold, freezing his brain and robbing him of his ability to sign. The cast members got in place and waited with held breaths as Mr. Phillips welcomed the guests. The curtains rattled open, and for the first time in his life, Benjamin was face to face with the biggest crowd he had ever seen.

The show opened with Captain Jack Sparrow, Will Turner and Elizabeth Swann. Will Turner was down on one knee, professing his love to Elizabeth and was trying to get her hand in marriage. A fearful Captain Jack Sparrow came bursting onto the stage, running and looking over his shoulders before disappearing again. The attention-grabbing scene was equally matched by the sound crew sending out calming sound of waves hitting the shores. Will and Elizabeth were frightened by Captain Jack's running and they too fled the stage. Benjamin's nerves were not completely settled but he had regained his ability to sign. The cameraman was alternating the video recorder from one end of the stage to the other. Benjamin extended his hands and held his head a little higher every time the camera light came his way.

Davy Jones' frightening image appeared on stage in all of his spine-tingling glory. Pirates screamed at his presence as he plundered their ships, sending them tumbling into the high seas. Jones dismounted The Flying Dutchman — his cursed ghost ship, and strolled to the front of the stage to deliver his nail-biting speech.

"Do you fear the unknown? Do you fear being forever casted into a bottomless pit? Cross me, Davy Jones and your soul will forever be lost." He held his head back and gave a bellowing laugh as the rest of the cast members joined him on stage to sing, "I'll tell you a tale of a pirate ship that plundered and tormented the seas…"

The audience gasped, laughed and sometimes clapped their hands in response to what was happening on the stage. The scene changed and Captain Jack Sparrow and the feared Davy Jones were left face to face. Benjamin waited for Davy Jones to speak for him to thrill the crowd with his sign language. The music was on and the director was giving the cue to go, but Patrick – Captain Davy Jones' face was the picture of every kind of nervousness.

"Patrick, you need to say your line," Imran whispered in desperation.

Patrick held his face with an absence of awareness, causing his eyes to slouch in their sockets. Imran whispered again but Patrick looked as good as dead. His unresponsiveness awakened something inside of Benjamin. He was familiar with Patrick's lines; in fact, Benjamin was familiar with everyone's lines. The audience was squirming in their seats and clearing their throats. The show was in danger and Benjamin was compelled to take responsibility. Taking on the role of Davy Jones was an unavoidable circumstance that Benjamin immediately dove into.

CHAPTER

17

Benjamin's father's lips widened across his face as he made himself comfortably seated on his son's bed in the wee hours of Saturday morning. Benjamin struggled to get his eyes open, a challenge caused by a combination of sleep and mucus. His father was dressed to go out, not dressed in his usual sweatpants and merino top he wore around the house, or the more appropriate pajamas considering the time of morning. They had not discussed the plan for the day which would have made his father's presence in his room rousing him out of his sleep understandable. Benjamin turned his head to the side and squinted at the little clock on his bedside table, its hands were pointing to 5 a.m. Benjamin thought it was unconscionable for his father to be present in his room at such an ungodly hour on a weekend morning.

"We have to get going Benny," his father kept on saying over and over as if they had made arrangements on being somewhere. In between his state of sleep and wakefulness, Benjamin was trying to remember if they had made any such plans. He rubbed his eyes and slowly raised his body to a sitting position on the edge of the bed beside his father.

"Go and have a shower," his father said, patting him on his shoulder.

His father's strange behaviour made him curious. Benjamin yawned widely and stretched his arms to a ninety-degree angle which caused his limbs to crack, releasing the overnight tension in his joints. He dragged himself to the bathroom to get ready for whatever plans his father had for the day. Before he got into the shower, Benjamin reached for the baby brush that he kept hidden at the back of the medicine cabinet and used the fine bristles to massage his chin and upper lip. This had become a part of his ritual to encourage the growth of his facial hair. He stroked his face then returned the brush to the hidden spot in the cabinet and immediately stepped into the shower without allowing the water to run for a few seconds. The water gurgled in the pipe before tumbling out with a choking thud. Benjamin made a small shriek as the cold water sprayed from the overhead pipe and hit his back.

His father had some warm milk waiting for him to which he added cereal in small amounts to prevent the crunchy flakes from getting soggy. Benjamin ate with cautious enthusiasm, not knowing what was waiting for him made him uneasy. The hum of the refrigerator was wiped out by his father's slurping of his mint tea. They were the only ones awake in the house, which made their early morning excursion even stranger. The house stood still in the cool morning air as the automatic garage door came to a close, marking their exit. The golden-streaked clouds announced the rising sun in the pale blue sky. They drove down the dew dampened hill, listening to the broadcaster on the radio speaking in the local dialect. Joggers had started their early morning trek, breathing heavily with their hands clutching their waists as they mounted the hill. At the foot of the hill, the fruit vendors were getting their stalls ready for the hustle and bustle of the day.

Benjamin rolled his window down, enjoying the fresh, cool wind caressing his face. The roads were mostly quiet except for a few stray dogs that barked and lengthened their legs in pursuit of the moving motorcar. Some parts of the city were more alive than other areas. Benjamin shook his head from side to side, refusing the advances of the newspaper vendors who were jostling to get to the car at the stoplight. They held their arms wide open, displaying the front-page headlines. Benjamin did not see the necessity for people to buy the paper version of the news when everything was so accessible on the Internet. The light turned green and his father drove away, leaving the vendors at the intersection still holding on to their papers. His father overtook a city garbage truck spewing thick black smoke from its mufflers. His father hissed through his teeth and complained about the gas emissions that were destroying the ozone layer.

As had become the norm, his father used their time together to educate him on politics, continents, accounting and topical issues in the news. He thought his father was displaying the same kind of hypocrisy that he came to associate with adults. Benjamin was brimming with curiosity, but his father's voice remained on the same monotonous tone as if nothing special was happening. Benjamin participated in the conversation halfheartedly, trying to keep his voice upbeat and optimistic, but he was disappointed. His father was not revealing what he really wanted to hear.

The sun was up and was making patterns of colour across the sky as they left the city behind. Benjamin extended the car visor to block the brightness of the sun that was bearing down heavily on him in the car. They stopped by one of the vendors who dotted the once empty roadsides with their Saturday morning pots of chicken-foot soup, boiled and roasted corn, peanut porridge, and egg sandwiches that they served in grease-drenched napkins. They bought roasted corn, the kernels of which they ate with small bites of husked coconuts. The combination of dried corn and sweet coconut made Benjamin thirsty, and he silently scolded himself for forgetting his water bottle. It was not a discomfort which he faced for long. His father was thirsty too and he made another stop at a gas station to get two bottles of ice-cold water.

Benjamin's state of full stomach and quenched thirst made him contented. He pried the sneakers off his feet, first using the front of his right shoe to push down on the back of his left sneakers, and then did the same with his bare toes on the back of the right shoe. He reclined the seat and folded his arms across his chest in readiness for a nap. His father rolled up the windows and turned on the air conditioner, an act he hardly did without complaining about the high cost of gasoline. The padded leather seat acted as a cushion against the numerous potholes along the winding country roads. Time stood still and the next thing Benjamin knew, they were parked outside a building with the name *Compassion Animal Haven* painted on the wall in blue and white.

Benjamin's spirit brightened. Being there could only mean one thing but as his mother often said, "If it seems too good to be true, then it's probably not true", and this seemed too good to be true.

They were met by a pleasant looking gentleman wearing a white shirt with the company's logo sewed into the left breast. He came through the sliding glass doors which had the opening hours and workdays printed on them in calligraphic letters. The man's movements were springy, he was waving and smiling as if he had been expecting them. The man and Benjamin's father called each other by their first names as they shook hands and patted each other on the shoulders.

"Mario, this is Benny," his father said, pointing to him.

Benjamin waved his hand awkwardly in response to the attention that was now focused on him.

"The boy has gotten big, last time I saw him he was this high." Mario was bent over with his hand at the height of his knees. He straightened his back, staring in disbelief at the much bigger version of what Benjamin had become. Mario's distended belly jiggled beneath his white shirt as he and Benjamin's father shared a laugh. Mario's shock did not last for much longer before he got down to business.

"Come this way," Mario said, pointing to the building he had exited minutes earlier.

Benjamin and his father greeted the secretary who was sitting behind a brown lacquered desk and was playing solitaire on her desk top computer. She raised her head briefly from her game and smiled at them. Benjamin observed that she was a woman who obviously thought moderation was overrated. She was wearing too much face powder, too much lipstick, too much weave, too many colours on her nails, and was chewing the gum in her mouth too loudly. She moved her mouth in wide open, circular motions and made loud chomping sounds as if there were no softeners used in the manufacturing of the chewing gum. Benjamin was expecting to be met with the pungent scent of animal faeces, but the only smell present was the strong scent of disinfectant from the still damp floor.

They were led outback by Mario and led into another building which had grey garage-style doors. The doors opened to a pack of floppy-eared, waggy tail dogs. There were dogs of every age, size, and breed housed in iron cages that were separated by guillotine doors.

"Have your pick," Benjamin's father said, smiling at him.

He opened his eyes in disbelief, not sure he was hearing what he was hearing. Benjamin removed his hearing aids and blew heavily on them to clear any possible blockages before putting them in his ears again. This caused the men to laugh. Mario handed him a folder which had the biography of every dog presently housed in the kennel to aid with his choice. He was in dog heaven. He moved slowly, going from cage to cage, gauging the connection he felt with each animal and reading from the folder what made them special.

His father and Mario were taking slow steps behind him. There were no Cane Corso or English Mastiff for him to choose from, but there was an Irish Wolfhound being housed separately in a glass enclosed area of the kennel that had running air conditioner. With its oversized body, it stood like a giant compared to the other dogs. It strolled powerfully behind the glint of the enclosure, displaying the well-developed muscles in its four legs and staring as if it wanted Benjamin to notice its superiority. He knew that a dog like this would surely be a threat to Norman, but there was no way his father was going to let him have that dog. His father and Mario joined him at the glass enclosure to stare at the dog that had curled its lip back and was baring its teeth. His father said it looked like the Irish Wolfhound was born with ten times the aggression of normal dogs. Benjamin walked away and went around the corner, back to the more realistic area of the kennel with regular iron cages.

His father and Mario came around the corner talking. "There is a growing fraction of new rich on the western end of the island who illegally import these dogs without thinking about the long-term care of them. If the government is not careful, they will start importing pet lions and tigers to act like they are in Dubai," Mario said.

Benjamin's father shook his head in the affirmative and was staring blankly as if he was worried about the possibility of being chased by pet lions and tigers around the island. The kennel was mostly quiet, except for a few sparing woofs here and there. There was a small brown and white mongrel dog that was keeping its eyes on Benjamin no matter where he went. Her biography stated her name as Prudence; a playful and obedient seven-week old pooch. Adopting a mongrel was the furthest thing from Benjamin's mind, but the cheerfulness she brought him made him change his thinking. He did not choose Prudence immediately. He did another loop around the kennel, re-examining every dog, except for the Irish Wolfhound. He came back to Prudence and felt the same fondness as he had felt before. She was the one.

"I want this one!" Benjamin called to Mario and his father, who were leaning against the wall having leisurely conversation.

Prudence was barking and wagging her tail as if she understood what was taking place. Benjamin's father leaned over the cage to examine her.

"Are you sure?" his father asked to which he nodded.

"Good choice Benny," Mario said.

Mario slid open the cage and removed Prudence and placed her in Benjamin's hands. She was small enough to nestle comfortably in the crevice of his arm. She was a sturdy puppy with an excessive layer of white fur with splotches of brown spots. His father used his cell phone to take a picture of him smiling and holding Prudence, who was slobbering Benjamin's hands. Since his impressive performance at the musical, he had been showered with gifts and praises, but getting Prudence was his best gift yet. He had saved the show by taking over the part of Davy Jones and he was being rewarded nicely for it. There was some paperwork that needed to be done inside the main office before they could leave with Prudence. Benjamin held her in his lap and stroked her head while his father filled out papers and signed documents in Mario's office. Benjamin felt pride in holding her and knowing that she was his. He was happy, adopting Prudence was an unusual occurrence in his unexciting life.

They did not immediately go home, his father brought him to a seaside restaurant at the pier. It was a homely looking building painted in bright Rastafarian colours with small, multicoloured bulbs hanging from the ceiling. The restaurant was brimming with tourists who were laughing loudly and speaking easily in their foreign accents. Benjamin ordered spicy chicken wings, cheesy fries and club soda. His father ordered a veggie burger with fries and orange juice. They sat outside at a metal table overlooking the sea. The sound of waves hitting against the canoes on the water's edge brought Benjamin peacefulness. They were being bothered by a few mosquitoes that were making haloes over their heads, but they remained seated on the patio. The view was beautiful, and Prudence was within their eyesight. She was tethered to one of the palm trees lining the entrance of the restaurant. She used her paws to scratch at the white-washed tree root playfully. It was a windy evening, and the breeze carried a plastic bag that became stuck to Prudence's face. She moved her body in crazed swirling motions until the bag became unstuck and blew away. The dog's antics were making Benjamin laugh. For being from an unsophisticated breed, Prudence was a bundle of joy he could hardly wait to show off to Winter and Oliver.

"Prudence sounds so humanly for a dog's name," Benjamin's father said.

He was leaned back in the iron chair with his hands resting at his sides. Benjamin thought about what his father said for about twenty seconds, but he liked the sound of the name. He liked the ease with which it rolled off his tongue when it was said.

"What's in a name?" Benjamin asked with a tone of sarcasm in his voice.

His father gave him one of those smiles that he usually gave when Benjamin had him cornered in a chess game. He did not mention anything else about the dog, and they sat staring at the scenic view in silence. The waitress, a medium-built woman, brought out their food to the table. Benjamin immediately started to eat his fries while they were still hot, and the melted cheese was still gooey on top of them. His father had this way of dividing the food in equal sections on his plate before he ate. He slowly divided his food and placed small bites in his mouth.

The mood his father had earlier left him. He was yawning and rubbing his eyes when they left the restaurant. Benjamin gently pulled the leash around Prudence's neck on the walk to the car and secured her in the plastic pet carrier his father had bought at the shop in the kennel. Evening shadows of the trees were retreating with the setting western sun. The city had begun to turn in for the day. Fishermen's canoes were docked on the shores with their nets glittering against the dark backdrop of the rippling water. The sounds of the Caribbean Sea grew fainter as they left the western city behind and approached the highway to Kingston. His father turned on the car radio, drowning out the sound of everything, even the whimpers of Prudence on the back seat.

Thomas was already asleep when they got home. Benjamin's mother tried to stroke Prudence, but she sneezed until tears ran down her cheeks when she picked her up. For the first night, Prudence slept on a pillow at the foot of Benjamin's bed. As much as he wanted to stay up and teach her how to fetch, Benjamin was too exhausted. He tried to turn off the light, but Prudence began to whine like a complaining child. Benjamin hated sleeping with the lights on but for Prudence's sake he turned back on the light and got into bed. It took less than five minutes for his room to be covered in a mixture of dog grunting and snoring.

The universe had a twisted way of sending trouble when you were least looking for it. The following morning, feathers from the pillow Prudence had slept on made Benjamin's bedroom floor look like someone had defeathered a chicken while he slept. There were bite marks and nibbles on the new pair of Adidas sneakers his grandparents had given him as a gift after his superb performance at the musical. Prudence was wagging her tail and staring innocently at what she had done. Her bold eyes made Benjamin unable to feel any type of anger towards her. He hid the sneakers beneath his bed and quickly gathered the feathers in a bag before anyone entered his room.

Thomas was standing and holding on to the coffee table for balance when Benjamin emerged from his bedroom with Prudence. Thomas shrieked at the sight of the dog and immediately let go of the table, plopping down on his diaper-clad buttocks. He turned his body on all fours and crept excitedly to where Prudence was sitting and gnawing on a piece of paper. Thomas was delighted to see the dog and was grabbing on to her tail too roughly. Prudence nipped at Thomas' hand in annoyance but missed. Not understanding the danger, Thomas was intrigued. He laughed, revealing his milk teeth and clapped his tiny fingers. Benjamin picked up Thomas and brought him to his highchair, out of the reach of Prudence. Benjamin filled Prudence's bowl with dry kibbles and placed it before him on the patio. He filled another bowl with water and placed it on the ground beside the dry kibbles. Prudence shoved her head into the bowl of kibbles and did not emerge until they were all gone. She moved over to the bowl of water, plunging her face inside it and curling her tongue backwards, lapping up the cool liquid. Benjamin's stomach was growling for the pressed green plantains and sautéed saltfish his mother was preparing in the kitchen. He wanted to eat, but his responsibilities to Prudence were of greater importance than his own stomach.

School came around and Benjamin was heartbroken to be leaving Prudence behind. He had dedicated his weekend to cleaning dog waste and doing dog care searches on the Internet. He woke up thirty minutes earlier than his usual time to carry out his obligations to Prudence. Benjamin got ready for school and secured Prudence to her leash for what was to become their daily walks to school. The nightingales fluttering over the vibrant neighbourhood gardens excited her. Benjamin held her leash tightly to prevent her from taking off after the birds. He rubbed Prudence's head before handing her leash to his mother when they got to the school gate. The affirmation for the day was, "I can do all things through Christ who strengthens me." His mother hugged him briefly before he walked away. He was heavy hearted and constantly looked over his shoulders at his mother tying Prudence's leash to Thomas' perambulator. Mr. Lewis was in the front garden wrestling with an overgrowth of shame-o-lady shrubs on the hibiscus flowers. Benjamin nodded in greeting and walked to the auditorium.

Students were gathered in small groups in the auditorium, talking gesticulatory. Benjamin went to the far end of the room and stood pensively staring at the stage. It had been a week since he had walked on the stage breathing heavily to be acknowledged for his role at the musical. At the time, Benjamin was nervous and was not sure what to do with his face as Mr. Phillips delivered his impassioned speech about embracing differences.

"We are proud to have a multitalented student like Benjamin at this school," Mr. Phillips had said. "What Benjamin did shows that we should accept and appreciate diversity." He was nervous on the stage, but also proud to be spoken of so highly.

Benjamin was reflecting on being acknowledged by the principal when a scraping sound on the ground startled him. He looked on the podium to see Mr. Lewis; he had entered through the backdoor and was attempting to center the lectern. He moved the wooden stand in alternating motions, pushing each side forward till it got to the center of the stage. Mr. Lewis walked from behind the lectern and went to the foot of the stage where he braced his torso backwards and squinted his eyes to judge the correctness of his effort. He jogged from the foot of the stage and back to the lectern where he twisted and turned the stand before running back to the foot of the stage again to judge his handiwork. He did this maybe three or four more times before he was satisfied with its position. He went to the back and returned with a spanking new bicycle with a matching red helmet swinging over the handlebars. He carefully leaned the bicycle against the lectern and waited in anticipation with outstretched hands before slowly walking away.

Mrs. Kennedy came in the auditorium, clapping her hands and ordering the students to get into their respective lines. Her silver whistle was gleaming around her neck, but for some reason, she no longer used it. The area for Benjamin's grade eight class was empty and he lingered about the room, first by pretending to be having a drink of water from his bottle, then by untying his shoelaces and retying them. He saw Lanay coming into the auditorium, pulling her bag on wheels behind her. She was struggling to balance her lunch bag and two books in the other hand. He wondered why no other student in grade seven ever seemed to be burdened with the number of books Lanay brought to school. Three teachers had joined Mrs. Kennedy and were directing the talkative students to their lines. The space for Benjamin's class line was still bare. He could not avoid the inevitable and went and stood in place at the front of the line, hoping the devotion would not be led by Mr. Bogle who had the habit of pointing to a student at the front to pray. He slid his heavy knapsack off his shoulders and placed it on the ground beside him.

The school day started like any other. More students slowly filed into the auditorium for the early morning devotion and announcements. Mr. Bogle - head of the English department- was wearing an old-style single-breasted suit with a peak lapel when he walked on stage to lead the devotion. He cleared his throat in the microphone and started singing a hymn loudly. He made his voice tremble to bring vitality to his sound, a practice which annoyed Benjamin when he was at church. He was not leading the devotion like a regular high school devotion, but more like a Baptist revival. As Mr. Bogle sung, his head began to shake violently. He spoke in unknown tongues as he spun his body in circles, hitting the bicycle Mr. Lewis had so carefully leaned against the lectern. The bicycle crashed onto the floor, causing the helmet to fly off the stage and land at the foot of the podium. A teacher who Benjamin saw often but never learned his name, picked up the helmet and tiptoed onto the stage with his back slightly bent and one finger pointing in the air. He picked up the bicycle amidst Mr. Bogle's spinning and turning, and rested it against the wall with the helmet unsteadily placed on the seat. Mr. Bogle dipped and dived on the podium and was still speaking in mysterious tongues. The students looked at him, not knowing when his possession with the spirit would end. But just as abruptly as he had started, he stopped. He straightened the glasses on his wrinkled face, took up the hymnal he had placed on the lectern, and walked casually from the podium, down through the lines and out through the door.

The students felt no surprise by Mr. Bogle's action. It was his tendency to become overcome with the Holy Spirit at odd times of the school day. In a jiffy, he could turn a simple lesson on nouns and pronouns, into a full-fledged fire and brimstone session. Mr. Bogle's shenanigans were quickly forgotten. The bicycle leaning against the wall on the podium was of more importance than anything that could have happened that morning. The light breeze fluttering over the room was making them cool despite the brightly burning sun outside. Benjamin had his eyes peeled to the stage looking at the bicycle and imagining himself riding down the hill with Prudence seated in a little basket in the space between the handlebars and the front wheel.

"I will be announcing the winner of the science competition."

Mrs. Ross' distinctive smile-sounding voice was about to bring an end to the students' curiosity, especially Benjamin's. She was unfolding a sheet of paper while holding the microphone to her mouth.

"The winner of the mountain bicycle is…"

She took a pause and held her head down, scanning the paper. She smiled subtly and repeated the sentence without revealing the name of the winner, bringing a theatrical feel to the announcement. She threw out more hints.

"The winner of the bicycle is a grade eleven student."

"The winner of the bicycle is extremely creative and inventive."

"The winner will go home today with a new bicycle and a matching helmet."

Benjamin's interest was piqued, and he was getting impatient with Mrs. Ross for fudging around with the answer.

"This year we had some exceptionally good entries," Mrs. Ross said. "The science department was challenged with choosing between two particularly good entries, although one of the two was a bit controversial. In the end, we chose the creator of the mobile robot. The winner of the bicycle is Marcus Bentley."

There was a short-restrained scream that came from one of the grade eleven lines. Marcus placed both hands on his head as he ran to the podium. Mrs. Ross was holding a certificate of achievement to be awarded to Marcus after a series of handshakes and smiles. He ignored her, leaving her standing awkwardly with her right arm extended for the handshake, and ran straight to the bicycle. He forced the helmet down on his head and jumped onto the bicycle. He sat on the seat with one foot flat on the ground, and the other on the pedal. He pushed down on the pedal, causing the bicycle to move forward. He rode around in circles on the stage, pedaling vigorously. The limited space on the podium was an impediment to his fun, so he dismounted and carefully pushed the bicycle down the steps to the auditorium landing. He adjusted the helmet on his head, got on the bicycle and pedaled up and down through the spaces between the class lines with one hand holding the handlebar and the other hand waving at his schoolmates.

After the excitement in the auditorium, the students went back to their classes filled with laughter and chatter. Melody was at the classroom door with a paper in her hand, looking in the direction of oncoming students. By the time Benjamin got inside the class, she had drawn a chair next to his desk and was waiting for him with an air of urgency on her face. What had made him worthy of her visit puzzled him. Benjamin clumsily caused his hand to hit his ear while removing his knapsack from his shoulders. His left hearing aid became partly dislodged from his ear canal and was squeaking loudly.

"What's that sound?" Melody asked.

She was speaking in the thick American accent that she had suddenly taken on after the musical. Benjamin was nervous and did not want to stutter, so he pretended something had gotten into his eyes. He adjusted the device in his ear canal and then used the sides of his hands to rub his eyes. Melody was looking at him, but she did not repeat the question. He pulled out his chair and sat down next to her. Her eyes were focused on his face and he looked away shyly.

"Benny, I will be running for president of the student council next year," Melody said.

He was surprised at the sound of his name; she had never called him by his name before.

"I need your commitment that you will be voting for me."

She had placed the paper on his table and was holding out a pen to his face. Benjamin could only nod his head in agreement, he did not feel like he had any other choice. Her campaigning for student council president was way too soon. It was early June and campaigning did not usually start until September, after summer break.

"Sign beside your name on the dotted line," she said.

Benjamin took the pen and scanned through the long list of names on the paper. He found his name and sloppily wrote B. Morgan on the dotted line beside it. Melody immediately took up the paper and walked over to Akeem who was sitting at the desk across from Benjamin's. There was no friendly pretense in her approach as she walked from desk to desk gathering signatures. She did so until Mr. Williams arrived in class, struggling to balance the test tubes and beakers in his hands.

The cashew tree in the front of the school yard was ladened with ripened yellow fruits. Instead of their lunchtime routine of going to the mango tree, Lanay and Benjamin went to collect cashew apples and their attached nuts. They poured tiny amounts of water from their bottles over the fruits, pretending it was enough to wash away any bacteria the fruits could have acquired before they ate them. They were careful not to make the staining juices fall onto their uniforms as they bit into the spongy, sweetish-sourish cashew fruits. In between eating, Benjamin gathered the rotten fruits in a pile for Mr. Lewis to collect later for his goat. Lanay's face was stained with the juice, and it made her look funny. She was filling her lunch bag with the cashew apples and handing him the nuts.

"Remember I should get some of the nuts when they are roasted," she said.

Benjamin nodded in agreement although he was not sure when his father would get around to helping him to roast them.

A heavy-set man came staggering past where they were under the tree, gathering the cashew fruits. There was a hot rage present in his red-tinged eyes.

"Where is Norman?"

"Normaaannnn!" the man called.

His speech was slurring, and he almost tripped over his uncoordinated legs. A group of curious students were beginning to gather around him as he carried on calling for Norman and cursing. Lanay left her lunch bag with the cashew apples laying in the dirt to watch the happenings. The man's voice was growing louder as he called for Norman.

"Yes…yes…daddy." Norman's voice was teetering on the border of fear and embarrassment.

"Come here to me boy," the man said.

The man staggered over to Norman who stood frozen in place. The man collared him and began to shake him mercilessly. Norman's body moved back and forth like he was the weight of a feather.

"Why don't you respect me?" the man asked. "How many times have I told you that you are too stupid for school?"

The man's stubby fingers were leaving dirt marks in Norman's forehead as he poked him. Norman stayed silent although his jaw was moving up and down as if he was grinding his teeth. The man started to punch him in his stomach, in the same way Norman had done to Benjamin weeks earlier. He started to breathe in a noisy, laboured way. His eyes rolled over, but his father remained consistent with the punching. The man let go off his grasp and Norman fell onto the ground sending up clouds of dust into the air. Benjamin's heart went out to Norman; he looked defeated laying fetus-like on the asphalted ground.

Even with Norman looking like he was at the verge of death, the man continued his assault. He stomped all his over body, leaving shoe prints on both his clothes and bare skin. Students stood wide-eyed and their mouths formed circles witnessing the attack on their schoolmate. There was thick blood streaming across Norman's face which was making a puddle on the ground, as the man kicked him without regard. It was in that moment, the other Benjamin Morgan was born. The two were unlike each other though they coexisted in the same space. He dropped the bag with the cashew nuts that he was holding, causing them to scatter in bouncing motions through the crowd. Benjamin did not allow himself to think before rushing over to the mayhem and laying on top of Norman, using his body to shield him from his father's strikes.

Benjamin had braced himself for an onslaught of blows, but only received a kick in his side from Norman's father's heavy boots before a faculty of teachers came on the scene and restrained him. The kick left a niggling pain in Benjamin's side, but it was nothing which required medical attention. Norman laid unconscious on the ground with his face badly bruised and swollen to the size of a pumpkin. Nurse Langley was called, and she came running, clutching her red and white first aid kit in her hand and wearing a stethoscope around her neck. She got down onto her knees and positioned her ears over Norman's mouth and nose to check his breathing. Although his stomach rose and fell, he remained unresponsive as Nurse Langley hastily unbuttoned his shirt and placed the stethoscope on his bare chest.

"Call an ambulance!" she shouted at the crowd gathered around her in a circle.

By now, Norman's full body had turned red and purple like an overripe starapple, replacing his original brown complexion. VP Doyle took his mobile telephone from his pocket and walked a few meters away where he placed a call and spoke gesticulatory with his back towards the crowd. His faithful dog was behind him and was looking as if he knew that something was terribly wrong.

"Go to your classes."

"I said go to your classes."

Mr. Phillips was desperately trying to send the students off to their classes, but each time they would take a few steps back and then loitered around until they were right back to where they had started.

It did not take long for the sound of 'wee-oww', 'wee-oww' to come bellowing up the hill. Someone from the office had pressed the remote, opening the gates for the ambulance to drive in. Norman's situation was assessed by the crew members after which he was strapped to a stretcher and taken away. After the ambulance left with Norman, a police car came and arrested his father who was locked away in the vice principal's office. He was shouting and swearing and looked as if he had wet himself as he was being led away to the waiting police car. Mr. Phillips guided one of the policemen to his office and shortly afterwards he came to fetch Benjamin for him to give a statement of what had happened. The policeman took a notepad from his breast pocket and began to write everything Benjamin said in painful detail. Someone was trying to whisper in the front office but had whispered too loudly that Norman had fractured some ribs. There was much condemnation of the brutality meted out to him by his own father. But there was also side talk and worry about the safety reputation at Saint Michael's High School. The school prided itself for its high wall fences topped with coils of barbed wire, and its world-class electronic gate almost as much as it prided itself for its spectacular external exam passes.

Benjamin gave his statement to the policeman who was wearing a floral shirt instead of the uniform of blue serge trousers with red stripes going down the sides, and blue and white striped shirt. Benjamin walked out of the room, locking the door quietly behind him. He was almost tiptoeing past the group of teachers and administrators gathered in the front office when Mr. Phillips stepped away from where he was standing at the secretary's desk and pulled him to the side. His hand felt cold, almost too cold for someone who was not handling items coming directly from a refrigerator. Lanay was waiting for Benjamin at the door and looked at him quizzically as if to say, "What now?"

"Good evening sir," Benjamin said before Mr. Phillips could say anything.

He immediately felt foolish. He felt like a fool for saying evening when it was just past afternoon, but he would have felt even stupider correcting himself.

"What you did today was very brave and selfless," Mr. Phillips said. "It is always good when we help people no matter how badly they have hurt us in the past."

Benjamin did not know what to say and stared blankly at the black and white tiles on the floor. He swallowed a ball of spit that had gathered in his mouth. Mr. Phillips was looking at him pensively, and he started to cough because he could not think of anything to say. Plus, he did not want to stutter. Mr. Phillips shook his nervous hand with one of his cold hands while using his free hand to pat Benjamin's shoulder. He released his hold and Benjamin immediately made a beeline for the door.

"Benjamin," the principal called out.

Benjamin turned around with a huge lump in his throat.

"The camera had all the answers," Mr. Phillips said, while raising an eyebrow and then smiling.

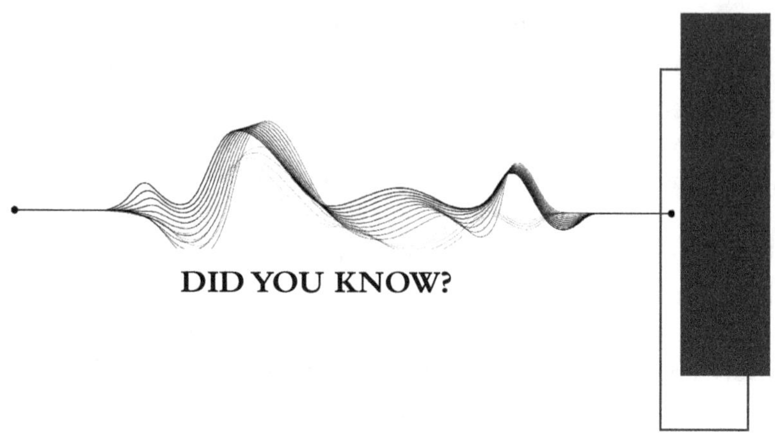

DID YOU KNOW?

Bullying can happen to anyone; however, evidence reveals that children who are considered 'different' are more at risk.

The United Nations Educational, Scientific and Cultural Organization (UNESCO) defines bullying as having three important components.

Repeated aggressive behaviour that involves unwanted negative actions.

Involves a pattern of behaviour repeated over time.

Involves an imbalance of power or strength.

Bullying behaviour usually targets difference.

Disabled young people and those with special education needs are significantly more likely to experience bullying than their peers. This phenomenon is called disablist bullying.

Disablist bullying might include: verbal, physical or emotional harassment, sexual harassment, insulting or degrading comments, name-calling, gestures, taunts, humiliation, exclusion, torment, ridicule, threats, manipulation, offensive graffiti, and refusing to work or co-operate with disabled children or those with special education needs.

LEARN BASIC SIGN LANGUAGE

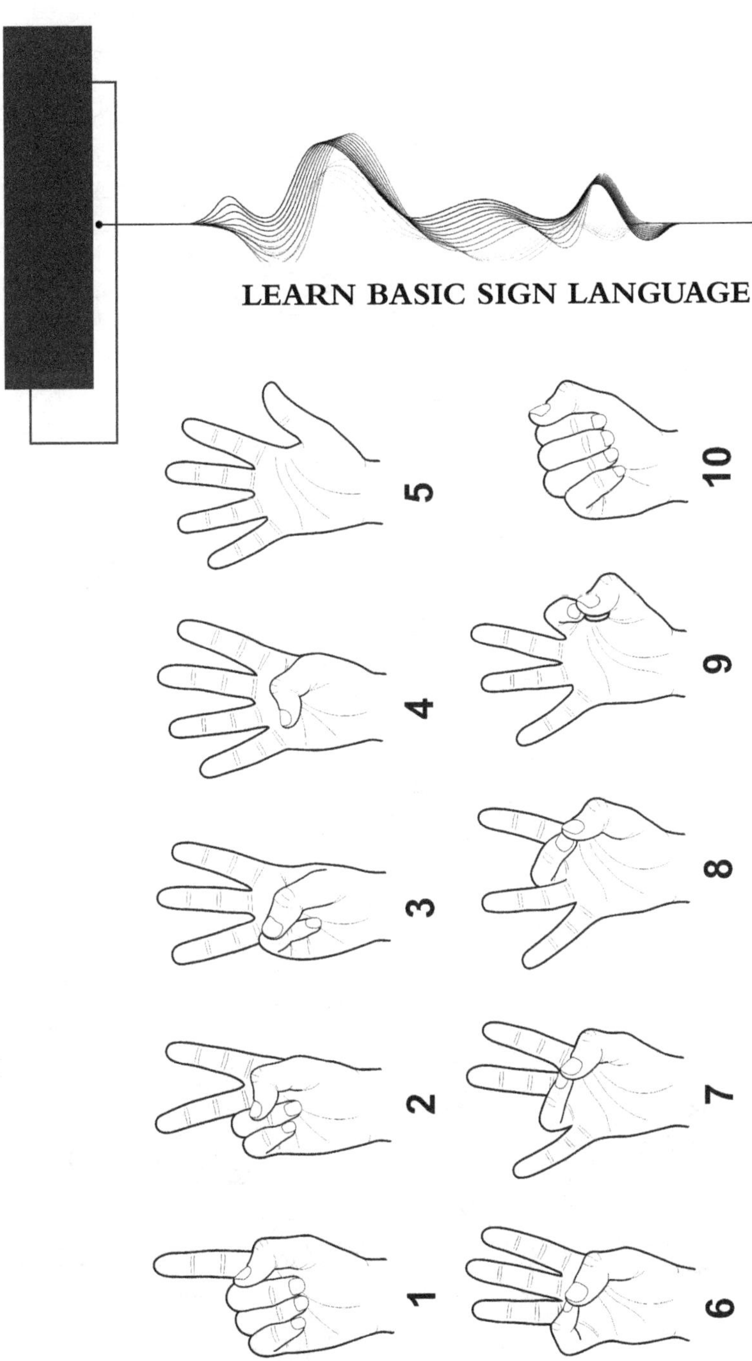

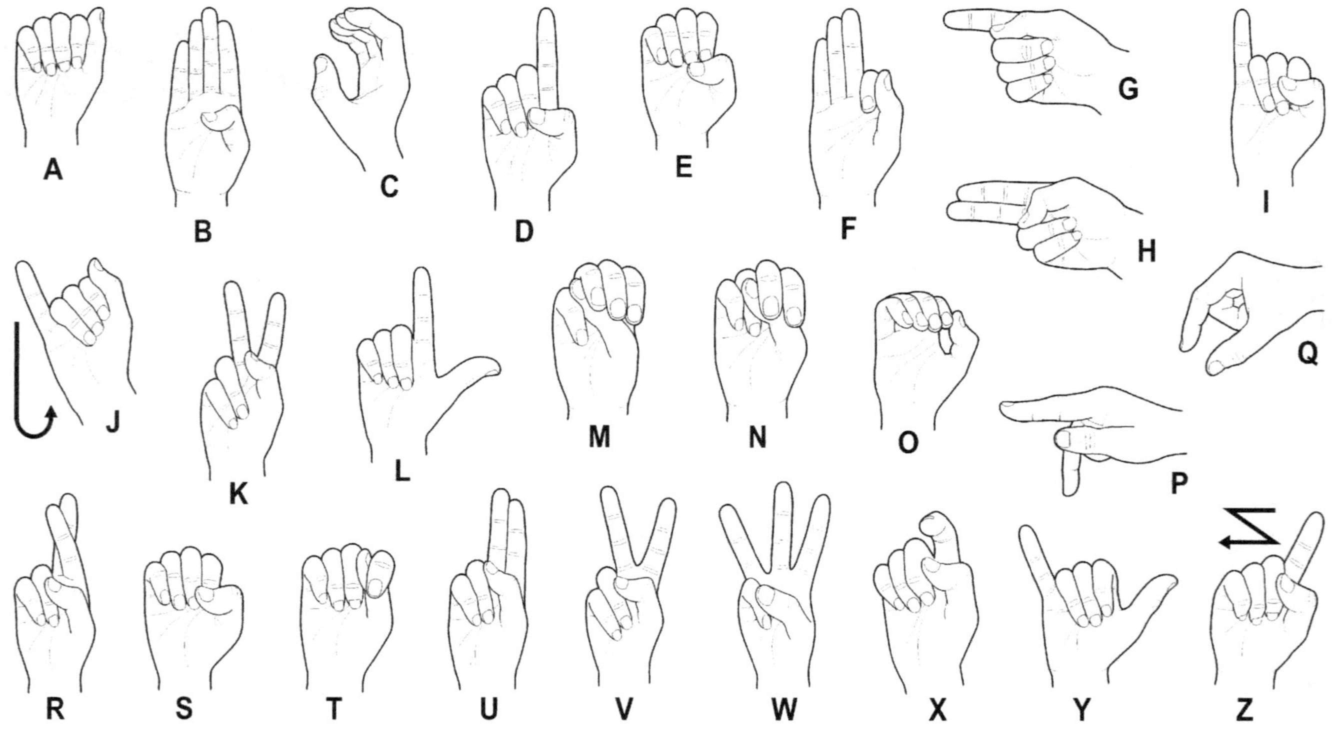

CPSIA information can be obtained
at www.ICGtesting.com
Printed in the USA
JSHW042304261122
33647JS00004B/11